$\mathcal{D}m$

# FOREVER AUTUMN

After a heartbreaking deception, Stephanie Gibson decides to change her life completely. She moves to the south coast to work as a nanny for the large and scatty Matthews family. Her employers are friendly and eccentric, and Stephanie soon settles in. She is enchanted by her charge, Nikki, and loves the challenge of her new job. However, when she finds herself falling in love again, spectres from the past loom up. Has Stephanie made another mistake and will she ever learn to trust again?

*Books by Christina Jones*
*in the Linford Romance Library:*

DANCING IN THE MOONLIGHT
LAVENDER LANE
HONEYSUCKLE HOUSE
SUMMER OF LOVE

CHRISTINA JONES

# FOREVER AUTUMN

*Complete and Unabridged*

**LINFORD**
*Leicester*

First published in Great Britain in 2001

First Linford Edition
published 2006

British Library CIP Data

Jones, Christina, *1948* –
    Forever autumn.—Large print ed.—
    Linford romance library
    1. Love stories
    2. Large type books
    I. Title
    823.9'14 [F]

ISBN 1–84617–529–1

Published by
F. A. Thorpe (Publishing)
Anstey, Leicestershire

Set by Words & Graphics Ltd.
Anstey, Leicestershire
Printed and bound in Great Britain by
T. J. International Ltd., Padstow, Cornwall

This book is printed on acid-free paper

# Part One

Part One

The falling leaves swirled and tumbled — russet, ochre, amber, gold — mingling with the pale pastel paper petals of the confetti in a multicoloured snowstorm. Beneath the overcast grey sky, the city church looked momentarily pretty. Shrugging deeper inside my jacket, I watched the top-hatted bridegroom and the bride with hair the same colour as the autumn leaves, pose for photographs before kissing one another and ducking, laughing, into their ribbon-bedecked limousine.

Then I turned and ran back quickly to the waiting taxi before anyone saw me and recognised me and thought me a sad voyeur.

The driver grinned over his shoulder as I closed the door. 'Friends of yours?'

'You could say that.'

He changed gear as the cab rejoined

the traffic. 'I'd have thought if they were real friends they'd have invited you. To the wedding.'

I sank back into my seat, delighted to be out of the chill September wind, and made myself return the grin. 'Well, not so much friends now, as people I knew in my past.'

'Get away with you!' He was talking to me through the driving mirror as the taxi stop-started through the busy streets towards the railway station. 'You're far too young to have a past. What time's your train?'

'Four o'clock.'

'Plenty of time then — despite your chosen route being a bit higgledy-piggledy and the unscheduled stop.' He tapped the rising meter. 'Not that I'm complaining, of course. You didn't plan the wedding detour by any chance, did you?'

Smiling, I shook my head and met his reversed stare with innocence. 'No . . . no, it was totally coincidental.'

Then I leaned back in my seat again,

and watched the familiar skyline crawl past. I'd lived in the suburbs of this Midlands city most of my life, and now I was leaving it forever. I smiled at the dramatic ring. Forever was a long, long time . . . Maybe not forever, then. After all, I was going to miss my parents very much, and although I'd made a lot of life-changes in the last few months, this one being the most radical, I'd still need to come home.

So, maybe one day, I'd return and pick up the threads of my old life . . . But not yet awhile. Not while I still felt such a fool.

I'd give it six months, I decided, sliding slightly on the leatherette upholstery as the taxi nipped round a corner. Six months at least before I came home. Six months in which time I'd have recovered the rest of my self-esteem, put the past behind me, and be able to hold my head high.

I closed my eyes and could see the bride and groom and the swirling leaves spinning faster and faster with the confetti snowstorm, and willed myself not to cry. I'd done all my crying ages ago. Well, most of it. The odd tear still somehow escaped when I least expected it. Hearing a piece of music, hearing a voice, catching a glimpse of a tall, fair haired man striding through the city streets . . .

And now, of course, seeing them as man and wife . . . Naturally I'd known from mutual friends when the wedding was going to be, and where. Everyone had assumed I'd avoid it like the plague. But I had to be there, to see it, to lay the final ghosts — and then to get as far away as possible. I'd timed my leaving to perfection.

'Wakey-wakey!' the taxi driver called cheerfully over his shoulder. 'Station coming up! You'll have plenty of time to sleep on the train.'

I quickly opened my eyes, forced another jolly smile, and nodded as the spread of the railway station loomed into view. It honestly couldn't come quickly enough for me.

The train was on time and thankfully not too crowded. I managed to find a window seat and several people helped me with my cases. Once everything was stowed in the luggage rack and under seats, I sat back and exhaled.

The railway journey to Bournemouth would take well over three hours, then there'd be a further taxi ride, so it would be dark when I finally arrived in Morton Hassocks. I liked the idea of that. Never having seen the village, it would give me something to look forward to in the morning, just in case this was, as everyone told me, the biggest mistake I'd ever made in my life.

I stared at my reflection in the streaky window as the train rattled away, heading south, leaving the grey windswept grimy streets of the Midlands city behind. My reflection, dark eyed, pale faced, too much unruly curly hair, stared confidently back. It would be all right — it would have to be all right. It was far too late to turn back now.

Richard and Lynne were husband and wife. My ex-fiancé and my ex-best-friend would live happily ever after. And me? I stared defiantly at my reflection as everyone around me settled down for the journey. I'd survive and find a new life and one day my heart would heal and the deception wouldn't matter at all.

The taxi journey from Bournemouth station was much quieter than my earlier one. Apart from me saying 'Hayfields Farm', 'Morton Hassocks' and 'please', and the taxi driver saying 'okay' and 'is this all your luggage?', the rest of the twenty minute trip took place in complete silence.

I stood outside the front door of Hayfields Farm, shivering in the darkness, watching as the taxi's tail lights dwindled away round a bend in the road, and wanted to go home. It was obviously true what they said — the travelling is far better than the arriving. I'd had no doubts at all until now . . .

Everywhere was shadowy dark, the

wind rattled through unseen trees and somewhere in the distance there was an incessant muffled roar like motorway traffic. The farm house was a bit of a plus, though, being, as far as I could see, straight out of a picture book — all mellowed brick, and odd bits of added-on buildings, and an uneven roof sloping against the autumnal night sky. There were lights spilling liquid gold out of nearly every window, and a dog barking from the depths of the walled garden, but I still wanted to go home.

However, before I could gather up my worldly possessions and turn tail and run, the front door was pulled open and Amanda Matthews peered out across the porch. 'Yes? Can I help you — ? Oh! Hi, Stephanie sweetheart!' She grabbed me, air-kissing me on both cheeks. 'You're early! Come along in . . . Is that all you've brought? Goodness, Peter would love you! I take masses whenever we travel — no, leave it in the hall, we'll take it up to your room later.'

I'd met Amanda only once before, at the interview in Birmingham. Then I'd been merely impressed that someone so much older than me could look so glamorous. Now the glamour was even more apparent and I was practically open-mouthed with envy. Bobbed blonde hair, size ten figure, expensively cut clothes and make-up straight from a magazine's beauty pages. I felt travel-grubby and incredibly scruffy in comparison, and surreptitiously tried to calm my curls.

'I'm terribly sorry, but we're going out this evening,' she said, leading me through a typical farmhouse hall — flagged floor, coat stands, wellington boots and a lot of old furniture buried beneath the day to day essentials of modern living — and into a huge, high-ceilinged living room. 'I do hope you don't mind . . . a social do of Peter's that came up at the last minute, and which he insists is vital for the business.'

I made a sort of soothing murmuring

noise. 'Oh, no — that's fine, of course. I mean, these things happen. I quite understand . . . '

Actually, three questions rushed into my brain at the same time: one — if they were going out was I expected to start my Nannying duties immediately?, two — did farmers actually have enough hours in the day to go out to impromptu midweek networking functions that involved so much dressing-up?, and three — why did the living room look as though someone had exploded something in the middle of it?

I must have been staring, because Amanda clapped her hand to her mouth and giggled girlishly. 'Don't say anything! It's my conversation opener!'

It didn't open any conversations for me, to be honest. I truly couldn't bring myself to exclaim 'Oh, my place is a tip, too!' or 'Goodness, I'll soon lick this into shape!'.

Amanda seemed to regain some sort of composure. 'To be honest — it's me being so lazy. We've been redecorating

11

in some of the other rooms and everything found its way in here — and never actually found its way back again. Putting everything away again is such a chore, isn't it? You have so much enthusiam for yanking it all out — but none at all for putting it back, don't you?'

I looked around at the piled-high clutter. Wasn't there anyone else in the house who could have lent a hand here?

She must have read my mind. 'No-one else would touch it. They all said I had to do it. Get focused, organised, stop procrastinating . . . ' she smiled at me beguilingly as if all these criticisms were pure virtues. 'And somehow I just never did it, and they wouldn't, so here it is . . . '

'There are jobs like that,' I admitted. 'Ones that are always best put-off until tomorrow — like cleaning the windows or clearing out cupboards or — ' I stopped. Okay, there really wasn't any comparison.

'You're very sweet, but I'm just bone

idle and easily distracted — as you'll probably soon discover. Now, the children are all out in the village tonight and won't be back until morning,' Amanda said, plonking herself down on a squashy sofa, pushing an entire rain forest of newspapers to the floor, and indicating that I should join her. 'We thought you'd prefer to have a quiet evening to settle in before being thrown in at the deep end tomorrow.'

*Children?* Plural? There had only been one child mentioned at the interview. I was still trying not to stare at the mess. My heart sank. My stomach, not wishing to be left out, rumbled.

'Oh, I'm so rude!' Amanda immediately stood up again. 'You must be starving! I mean, just because we're going out to supper and the children are being fed elsewhere doesn't mean that you won't want something to eat — I was going to sit here and have a cosy chat while Peter dolls himself up — answer any questions, you know

— but we can do that just as well in the kitchen. Come along . . . '

'I don't want to be any bother,' I muttered, also standing up and feeling hideously embarrassed. 'I'm not that hungry, honestly — I had a sandwich on the train.'

'Hours ago, no doubt,' Amanda was gliding through the hall again with me in her wake. 'Anyway, it'll be useful to be in the kitchen while we talk. You can get a feel for it. You'll probably spend a lot of time in here.'

Would I? Cripes . . . I looked round. The kitchen was large enough to swallow a semi-detached house whole and still have room for a conservatory. The ceiling was beamed, the floor quarry tiled, and everywhere else was limed oak. I couldn't remember if I'd agreed that cooking was to be part of my duties. I hoped not. I'd never find my way round all those cupboards without a route map.

Like the hall and the living room, the kitchen was fairly chaotic. There were newspapers and magazines strewn everywhere, while pens, crayons, children's toys and discarded clothes littered the surfaces. Amanda Matthews was no housekeeper. I wondered why she didn't employ a cleaner. Maybe that would become part of my routine, too. Nanny, cook, cleaner, servant-of-all-trades? I pushed the panic quickly away.

With amazing swiftness, Amanda flicked open cupboards, disappeared into walk-in larders, delved into fridges, and had the makings of a big enough ploughman's lunch to feed a rugby team on the table almost before I could blink.

'White wine? Red wine? Beer? Soft drink? Tea? Coffee?'

'Oh, er . . . wine, please . . . white . . . thank you.' I stood closer to the range — a real one, old cream enamel, with chipped bits showing the black beneath — and looked at the proliferation of vegetables and herbs, boxes and boxes of eggs, and racks of wine of every hue. Onions and garlic and more

15

herbs hung like dried flowers from the beams, and zillions of pots and pans and utensils swung from a sort of clothes-airer contraption above the double stone sinks. 'You must love cooking.'

'Can't stand it,' Amanda poured two glasses of wine and indicated that I should sit at a clear corner of the vast table. 'Never touch it. If food doesn't come microwaveable then I don't buy it. That's why you've got a ploughman's. My speciality. The kids do the cooking. Take after their father.'

The kids, I thought, must be pretty precocious. I sat down and started on the ploughman's. It was gorgeous — a huge salad, fresh crusty bread, real golden butter and cheese that crumbled under the knife. 'This is lovely — thank you. Oh, so — um — Peter — cooks, does he?'

'No! Whatever gave you that idea? Oh, no — sorry! No, my first husband was the chef — he passed on the culinary genes. Peter is my second husband and a worse cook than I am.'

I was concentrating on a particularly spicy pickled onion and hoping I'd eventually untangle the Matthews family ravels, when someone tried to batter down the back door.

'Oh, heavens! Dogs! Sorry — let them out hours ago — poor mites. Excuse me!' Amanda downed her wine in two gulps, and immediately jumped to her feet and disappeared round a Welsh dresser.

No wonder she was so slim, I thought, piling butter on to my bread, she never stayed still for a minute. A blast of chill air whooshed round my feet and there was much cooing and scrabbling of canine claws and then Amanda, preceded by three large shaggy dogs, reappeared.

'Rescued lurchers. Spot, Fido and Rover — no, not really! Zola, Gus and Gi-Gi — and oh, good, they seem to like you.'

They did. They were all attempting to sit on my lap at the same time. It was like being crushed by a pack of very affectionate wolves.

'Push them off if you want to, they won't mind.' Amanda poured herself some more wine. 'Now, ask me whatever you want to. Anything at all.'

'Well,' I'd managed to extricate myself from the dogs who were now resting their chins on the table and staring covetously at my ploughman's, 'when you interviewed me in Birmingham, I thought you said you had one child and — oh, my goodness!'

'What? *What?*' Amanda's voice rose in panic, then she followed my eyes and giggled again. For someone of her age, I thought, she giggled a lot. 'Oh, yes — my boys — gorgeous, aren't they?'

My eyes were riveted on a photograph on the middle shelf of the dresser. Two of the most beautiful men I'd ever seen smiled sexily back at me. They were both wearing faded cut-off jeans and nothing else, both looking up from hauling some sort of small fishing boat up a beach — with a lot of blue sea in the background.

'Joel and Lucas — Joel's the dark one, two years younger than Luc. Taken on the beach here last year. Had to take the snap. Don't often get them in the same place at the same time.'

'They're your *sons*? But I'm here to look after your child — er — children . . . '

Amanda spluttered through her wine. 'Not the boys! Sorry — I really should have explained. Joel's thirty and Lucas is thirty two. I don't think they'll require a Nanny — although they may well enjoy having you around. No, they're my sons from my first marriage. Peter and I have Nikki . . . ' She pointed to another photograph of a little blonde girl, maybe four years old, and looking like a fairy doll. 'You'll be looking after her for the three months of my contract . . . Little angel, isn't she?'

I murmured my assent. Nikki was certainly beautiful, but I'd learned over the years that the old adage of handsome is as handsome does was very true — particularly where children were concerned. And if Joel and Lucas were thirty somethings, that meant that Amanda was even older than I thought she was.

She laughed, as though reading my mind. 'I've had my babies at either end of the biological scale! I married my first husband when I was sixteen — and I'd had both Joel and Lucas by the time I was eighteen. Quite a shock to the system I can tell you. Then Nikki came along totally unexpectedly four years ago — just when I thought my baby-making days were long gone and HRT beckoned.'

I did lightning mental calculations. Amanda Matthews was forty eight, then ... Twenty years my senior. I only hoped I looked half that good when I reached her age.

We talked about my duties for a while as I finished eating and the dogs fell asleep on my feet. The bare bones of the job had first leapt at me from the magazine advertisement, and the rest we'd covered at the interview, of course, and there had been a proper contract drawn up and my references had been checked out and we'd both been more than happy.

Amanda had, at some time, been an actress with a repertory theatre company which had long since disbanded. They'd apparently re-formed for a one-off sentimental reunion, and would be playing at a theatre in Bournemouth until Christmas, with rehearsals starting at the end of September. Two shows a day, five days a week and a Sunday matinée. Amanda hadn't wanted to turn it down, and three months away from my previous existence had seemed like a lifeline.

'The offer of the play has been a wonderful ego boost,' Amanda said now, refilling our wine glasses yet again. 'And meeting up with the old crowd has been brilliant — the years simply fell away. But I thought I'd have to turn it down because of Nikki. She starts school after Christmas, but there are no nursery places available short-term and I didn't want to farm her out. So you — ' she leaned across the table and patted my hand, 'are a gift from the gods.'

I only hoped she'd think so when I'd actually started work. However, there was no time to voice any doubts, as the dogs all rumbled in their throats, then wagged their tails in perfect timing, and a tall man in a tuxedo wandered into the kitchen.

'Hi . . . ' he grinned at me. 'You must be Nanny.'

'Stephanie,' Amanda reproved. 'Stephanie, this is Peter, my husband.'

He was probably ten years Amanda's junior and handsome in a television advert sort of way. He shook my hand gravely. 'Welcome to the madhouse, Stephanie. I hope you'll soon feel like one of the family.'

'Amanda — er — Mrs Matthews has already made me feel very much at home, thank you.' I blinked at Peter's evening dress glamour. He certainly didn't look like my idea of a farmer. But then, being the archetypal townie, what did I know? 'And I'm really looking forward to meeting Nikki.'

'She can't wait to meet you, either,' he smiled, pouring himself a glass of wine and glancing at Amanda. 'Just the one, darling, I know — I'm doing the driving tonight.'

Amanda stood up again. 'Actually, we'd better be off — Stephanie, let me show you to your room — Peter can bring up your bags. Then we'll leave you in peace.'

⋆ ⋆ ⋆

Half an hour later, they did just that. My room was in the attic — I'd winced a bit when they'd told me: I could see a sort of Jane Eyre scenario unfolding — but I needn't have worried. It was, of course, glorious. A huge, vast loft conversion, with a double wrought iron bed complete with patchwork bedspread, a little lounge area including sofa and television, and a bathroom to die for, all with sloping windows in the roof and white rugs on the polished floorboards.

After I'd unpacked, had a long bath — lying back in the silky water staring at the blackness of the sky above my head — and watched something mindless on the television, I went to bed. I didn't imagine for a moment that I'd sleep. I'd eaten far too much, it was all so strange, and anyway I hadn't slept properly for months.

I tugged back the bedspread and duvet and clambered in — immediately sinking into a mattress of feathers. I had never experienced anything like it. The billowing softness cuddled me as I curled into a ball, the worries floated away, my eyelids, aided by the wine, felt heavy, and within minutes I was asleep.

★　★　★

I opened my eyes. My whole body was swaddled in a cosy, warm cocoon

. . . Where on earth was I? I squinted at the diffused golden light pouring through the skylight above my head. It certainly wasn't my bed . . . this wasn't my room . . . and what on earth was that noise? An unceasing roar that I'd heard before . . . last night when I'd arrived at — oh my God!

I sat up quickly and peered at the clock. I'd slept all night for the first time since — well — for the first time in ages! And this was my first day at work and now I'd probably overslept! Had there been any arrangements made? Was Nikki being fetched back from the village at the crack of dawn? Was I supposed to serve her a nourishing breakfast at a set hour? It was nearly half past eight and probably the whole of Hayfields Farm had done a day's work by now!

I flew into the bathroom, tore back to the bedroom, scrambled into a pair of jeans and a sweater, and hurtled downstairs.

I hadn't realised last night just how

many stairs there were to hurtle down. At least flour floors of them. At every step I expected Amanda or Peter to appear and ask me where the devil I'd been. Mercifully, I met no-one on my downward journey. The whole farm-house was silent — no doubt everyone was out tilling the soil or whatever it was that kept farmers so busy.

I skidded into the kitchen to be greeted by the dogs who were all desperate to be let out. Noticing that nothing had been touched from last night — the remains of my supper and the wine glasses were exactly where we'd left them — I negotiated the kitchen maze and unbolted the back door.

The dogs flew out in a rush of grey shagginess and I caught my breath.

The mist was rolling towards the farmhouse, melting beneath the early morning September sun in a gold and silver cloud: hovering just over the dipping fields, swirling between colon-nades of chestnut trees and trickling between the crumbling bricks of the walled kitchen garden. The sky, brilliantly blue, was far bigger than at home, and on the horizon it paled to infinity as it melted with — of course! The sea! That puzzling roaring, rushing noise was the constant ebb and flow of the ocean.

I stood, entranced. I'd never seen anything quite so beautiful in my entire life.

'Shut the door — it's freezing in here!'

The voice snapped me out of my 'season of mists and mellow fruitfulness' reverie. I stepped back into the kitchen, obediently closed the door, and gawped at the man standing in the middle of the floor.

'Who the hell are you?' His dark eyes widened.

'Stephanie Gibson.' I tried not to stare, which was pretty tricky as he was only wearing a very small towel and was wet with spiky black hair and totally gorgeous. And I had the advantage: I knew who he was, although his photo hadn't begun to do him justice. Joel — the younger son. 'I'm Nikki's Nanny.'

He clutched the towel closer round his waist. 'God — I'm so sorry. I thought you were Ma — she's usually messing about with the dogs in the morning, although it's a bit early for her, and — um — I mean, I wouldn't have shouted like that if I'd known and — er — would you like a cup of coffee?'

'Love one. Oh — shall I . . . ?'

He nodded. Obviously the making and pouring of coffee was going to prove fairly difficult while both his hands were occupied with the towel. 'I'll — um — go and get dressed . . . just got out of the shower . . . er — nice to meet you. I'm Joel Matthews.'

I smiled. I didn't want to say I knew. To my surprise he didn't head off in the direction of the hall and staircases and bedrooms, but made for a skew-whiff corner and stepped in between two of the floor-to-ceiling cupboards. I busied myself with the coffee pot and a couple of mugs and thought that if my employer's son chose to get dressed in a corner of the kitchen then it was really no concern of mine. The entire family set-up seemed a little — shall we say — off the wall — and I hadn't even met Nikki yet.

I plonked the coffee mugs on the table and cleared the debris of last night's feast on to one of the myriad draining boards. No doubt in time I'd locate waste disposal and dishwasher and everything else needed to make the kitchen a bit more respectable.

Joel reappeared from between the cupboards, wearing jeans and a rugby shirt, but still had nothing on his feet. This wasn't good. I'd always had a thing about men's feet, you see. Found them very attractive. Or at least, I used to. Joel's feet were the best — long, slender and suntanned and I tore my eyes away.

He picked up the coffee mug. 'Thanks for this. You must be the first one up this morning — I know Ma and Peter went to some shindig last night, so you probably won't see them until lunch time. Still, I don't have to be at work until half eleven, so I'll be able to run you into Morton Hassocks to collect Nikki from Lucas. Unless you've got a car?'

I sipped my coffee, working out the convolutions. Joel still lived at home on Hayfields Farm, Lucas didn't. 'No, I haven't. I sold my car when — er — well, I sold it. Amanda said there'd be a car here that I could use.'

'There is — not much of one but it goes — just. It's at Lucas's. You can collect it when you pick up Nikki — then I can go straight to work.'

'So you don't work with Peter on the farm, then?'

Joel spluttered into his mug. 'Me? God forbid! I'm a chef at the Bat and Broomstick in the village. And Peter doesn't spend any time working on the farm, either. He wouldn't know one end of a tractor from the other. He runs his own computer software company in Bournemouth.'

Which would explain the glamorous dressing up networking soirée, but sadly did away completely with my mental picture of rustic sons of the soil.

'So, um, is Amanda — I mean, your mother — the farmer? In between being wife, mother, and actress?'

He shook his head. 'No-one farms from Hayfields any more. Ma rented all the fields out to neighbouring farmers years ago. She retained the farm house and some of the outbuildings and enough land for her to have a good sized garden, and there's a bit of ground behind the veg patch where she keeps a few hens — just for the eggs.'

'Oh, right.' It was beginning to make a bit more sense.

'Dad played at farming before he got bored and decamped with the landlady from the Bat and Broomstick while Luc and I were still kids. But actually Hayfields belongs to Ma, it was her parents' place, she grew up here and so did we. Peter is the incomer.'

I looked up quickly. Was there just the tiniest inflection of bitterness in his voice? It seemed to suddenly occur to both of us that we were straying a bit too close to things that shouldn't involve me at all.

Joel swirled his coffee. 'So? What about you? I know Ma came back from Birmingham raving about you as though she'd discovered another Mary Poppins. She'd scoured the country to find the right person to look after Nikki while she does this play. We didn't think anyone would be good enough for her — so you must be Super Nanny.'

'Not at all.' I blushed. It was irritating, but it always happened. 'And there's not much to tell about me, really. I've lived just outside Birming-ham most of my life, been an inner-city primary school teacher for the last seven years, and wanted a change.'

Joel raised his eyebrows. 'Some change! What on earth made you want to leave the bright lights and bury yourself away in the heart of the country?'

I pushed the image of Richard and Lynne and the swirling confetti firmly out of my mind. 'Oh, you know . . . the feeling that time was passing me by and that I'd been in the same job and the same place for ever . . . '

Joel laughed. 'Pull the other one! This seems like a bit of a retrograde step to me.'

'Not at all. I've just reversed the running away to find out if the city streets are paved with gold scenario.'

'You're not kidding! The streets of Morton Hassocks are paved with far more fundamental stuff.'

I laughed. I liked a man who could make me laugh. Richard, with hind-sight, rarely had.

'Go on then,' Joel was still poised with his coffee mug. 'So you decided you'd had enough of being a city girl — then what?'

'Well, I'd resigned from my last school at the end of the summer term and was just hoping that something would turn up. Then I saw Amanda's advertisement and applied without even thinking that I'd be suitable . . . '

'So you've never even been a Nanny before?'

I shook my head. 'I reckoned that after years of ruling classes of over thirty children, then looking after one should be no problem.'

'Oh dear, oh dear — how wrong can you be? You haven't met Nikki yet! Maybe when you have, you'll change your mind and want to go home.' Joel met my eyes over the rim of the coffee mug and smiled. 'But I really do hope that you won't.'

'Well, yes, so do I.' I held his gaze. I had a feeling that I was being tested here. I really wanted to pass with flying colours. 'And is there any reason why I should?'

The silence seemed to last forever. 'I just think that you may well have some hidden agenda. You know, some other reason for being here, a reason that might make you want to leave.'

'I really have no idea what you're talking about. I've told you why I'm here — my job is to look after Nikki — nothing else.'

Joel grinned at me. 'Whatever you say — but I think you'll soon discover that Nikki isn't the only one in this family that needs looking after. I'd better warn you — your coming to Morton Hassocks is definitely going to be a rite of passage in more ways than one . . . '

# Part Two

Part Four

I refused to be fazed about meeting Nikki. I'd come this far. I wasn't going to be put off now. She could be the Child Monster from the Deep Lagoon and I'd still have a go at looking after her. Nor did I want to become embroiled in the Matthews' family secrets. It was far too soon in my plans for a new life to think about giving up.

And more importantly, I had absolutely no intention of telling anyone about my past or falling into the deadly trap of being flirted with by Joel. That was the quick route to heartbreak — and one I had no intention of ever travelling again.

Avoiding looking at the tantalising sun-tanned feet, I returned Joel's smile with a confidence I certainly didn't feel. 'I'm sure the rest of you are old enough to look after yourselves but the sooner

Nikki and I meet the better.' I spoke in my best school-mistressy voice. The one that usually barked 'Stop talking! Now!' 'And before we go, shall I wash up or does Amanda — your mother — have someone who comes in?'

'Does it look like it?' Joel laughed, not seeming at all put out that I'd changed the subject. 'Ma likes to think she's the best housewife and mother in the world. She's actually neither, although we love her to bits and we'd never let on. Peter isn't here often enough to notice the mess, and we're used to it. She's tried having cleaners in, but she'd never let them do anything — she'd just make them sit at the table all day drinking coffee and gossiping. She'd love you for ever if you just stuck the stuff in the dishwasher. It's usually my job. Or Lucas' when he's here.'

I saw to the dishwasher while Joel disappeared into the kitchen corner again and reappeared with the feet covered with trainers.

'Shall we lock up? Get the dogs in?' I

asked as he extricated his car keys from a jumble on one of the dressers.

'No — why?' He smiled that smile again as I followed him out into the yard. 'Oh, right — in case of urban terrorists? No, we never bother with anything like that round here. No-one locks their doors during the day.'

His car was an open-topped jeep. A rather old and battered and mud-streaked dark red jeep, and we tore away round the bend from Hayfields Farm with gay abandon. The chill wind tugged at my curls and the smell of the sea was everywhere. Conversation was limited owing to the noise and the gale so I clung on to the sides of my seat and was aware of tall trees and high-banked lanes and miles and miles of fields whizzing past in a flash.

It seemed the journey was all over in less time than it takes to ride a big dipper. Hayfields Farm, it appeared — although of course I'd missed it on my arrival last night in the darkness — was on the very edges of Morton

Hassocks. Morton Hassocks seemed to consist of half a dozen houses, the same number of cottages, both ringed by towering semi-naked chestnut trees, and a village green that looked as though it should constantly echo to the thwack of leather on willow.

As Joel slowed the jeep to a more normal speed, I realised that there was more to the village than initially met the eye. There was a small shop, the pub — the Bat and Broomstick, which was all whitewashed walls and black timbers — and a two-pump garage with one pump marked 'tractors only'.

The jeep stopped without warning outside a lean-to. Joel looked across at me. 'This is Luc's place. Baptism of fire time. Are you sure you're ready?'

'As I'll ever be,' I said brightly, wondering why Lucas lived in a shed.

Before I had time to wonder any more, the front door of the lean-to opened and the second man from the photograph appeared. Fair haired and dark eyed, he was absolutely stunning.

'Nikki's been awake since five,' he yawned, striding through piles of fallen leaves towards the jeep. 'Couldn't wait to meet the brave lady who is going to try and keep her under control.'

Hoping that this was just an attempt at sibling humour, I smiled. 'Well, here I am . . . '

Lucas gave me an appraising stare. 'And very nice too.' He grinned at Joel. 'Ma didn't say that she was quite so . . . '

'No, she didn't, did she?' Joel had slid from the jeep and opened my door for me, which I thought was charming of him. There are times for strident feminism and this wasn't one of them. 'Probably didn't want Peter getting overexcited. Stephanie, this is Lucas. Luc, Stephanie — oh, and Charlotte.'

'But I thought your sister was Nikki?'

'She is, but this is Charlotte.' Joel indicated a thin girl of about my age with long dark hair in an untidy bundle on top of her head, and wearing jeans and huge baggy sweater, peering through the doorway of the shed. 'Luc's wife.'

'Oh, right — ' I stretched my smile in an attempt to take in all the newcomers.

Lucas and Charlotte smiled back at me, but didn't look at one another. The smiles weren't convincing. It was as if we'd arrived in the middle of a domestic tiff or something.

'And this —' Joel said, 'is Nikki — hi, poppet!'

A tiny blonde whirlwind skimmed through the leaves, ducked through the mass of legs and hurled herself in Joel's arms.

Nikki had inherited all her mother's beauty, I thought. At four she was gorgeous — in twenty years time she'd have broken a million hearts.

'Hello, Nikki.' I grinned at her in what I hoped was a friendly and relaxed manner. 'I'm Stephanie. I've been dying to meet you.'

'Hello,' she looked at me from under long eyelashes. Her eyes, like her half-brothers', were the darkest navy blue. Almost black. 'Are you going to teach me things?'

'I'm going to look after you, and take you out, and play with you, and I can teach you things if you'd like me to. Why?'

'Because Mummy said you were a teacher. And teachers teach.'

No flies on Nikki, then. 'We'll do whatever you want to do when we've got to know each other. Shall we go and get your things and go back to the farm, then you can show me your room?'

'Okay.' Nikki struggled in Joel's arms, scrambled down, and tore back into the lean-to.

'Fifteen-love to you so far,' Joel said, as he watched Nikki scamper away. 'Ma and Peter have spoiled her rotten — so this is the lull before the storm, I'd say. Will you be okay getting back to Hayfields?'

I nodded. I guessed the dilapidated green Mini which was, like Charlotte, probably the same age as me, was the promised car-with-the-job. And I couldn't see myself getting lost on the half a mile journey back to the farm.

'Come in and have a cup of coffee before you go,' Lucas said, without, I thought, much enthusiasm.

Charlotte, who had been almost lurking in the doorway, shook her head. 'We haven't got any milk, Lucas. Nikki had the last with her cereal. And as we haven't paid the last milk bill, buying any more isn't an option.'

'Black's fine for me,' Joel said blithely, 'and for Stephanie.'

Now normally I prefer to be asked before someone makes a decision for me, but the undercurrents were getting very strong. I smiled again and followed Joel along the leaf-strewn path. My face, I felt, would ache from cheery smiling long before we'd left the lean-to.

The inside of the shed was a revelation. One long building, divided into tiny rooms by clever use of book cases and plants and screens, it glowed with colour. The roof sloped, the walls bulged and beneath the various rugs, the stone floor dipped and swayed. But it was a charming and original home, and thanks to a huge log burning stove, wonderfully snug on this brisk autumn morning.

'Please sit down,' Charlotte indicated a long, low sofa covered with coloured throws as Joel and Lucas busied themselves at the kitchen end. 'And I hope you don't mind the cats' hairs.'

'Not at all,' I plonked myself down. 'We've got three at home. At my parents' home, I mean. This is a lovely house.'

Charlotte looked at me closely. 'You mean it?'

'Yes. It's so cosy and — well, bright and warm and — um — different . . . '

'It's certainly that!' When she laughed, Charlotte's thin face was animated for the first time, and she looked pretty and alive. 'It was all we could afford. Luc's mother was a bit put out I think, and

47

would have loved to have seen us in a mock Tudor with integral garage. But we didn't want handouts to buy a semi on an estate — we wanted to finance our own home, or at least Lucas did, so this is it.'

I could understand that. I'd have felt the same. And to be honest, if you were going to be sharing with someone as drop-dead gorgeous as Lucas, then a tent on a windswept cliff top would have seemed like heaven.

Lucas and Joel and coffee arrived from one end of the lean-to at that point, and Nikki and her overnight bag from the other, so if Charlotte had been going to expand on any further Matthews' family secrets, the moment was annoyingly lost.

Once coffee was over, the rudiments of the Mini's temperamental behaviour was explained to me, then with Nikki installed in her back seat harness, Charlotte, Joel and Lucas waved us goodbye.

'I like you,' Nikki piped over my

shoulder as we made the return journey to Hayfields in a much more sedate fashion than my earlier trip in Joel's jeep.

'Do you? That's lovely. I like you, too.'

'I like your hair. Charlotte's hair is nice too, but not as nice as Mummy's.'

I smiled to myself. What a sweet child! I couldn't imagine why Joel had thought she'd be as problem. He should have faced some of the junior monsters that I'd had to deal with in my classrooms!

'I don't like Charlotte's hair up, though, do you? Charlotte only puts her hair up when she's with Lucas. When she's with Daddy she lets it hang down.'

The Mini nearly veered off the road! I concentrated hard and managed to stay on course. Surely not! Still, what did they say? Out of the mouths of babes . . . I wondered wildly just what sort of set-up I'd walked into. Of course these things happened — but I sincerely hoped they weren't happening here! Charlotte and Peter? Oh heavens — talk about keeping it in the family!

Still, Joel had said Nikki wasn't going to be easy. Maybe this was what he'd meant. Maybe she had a very fertile imagination and told trouble-making whoppers. I nodded to myself. I could cope with that, and deal with it, too. I'd experienced it before in school and knew that it often happened with only children — which Nikki was, really, given the huge age-gap between her and her half-brothers.

Nikki broke off in the middle of humming a Steps song. 'Belinda's got the best hair though. Better than yours or Charlotte's or Mummy's.'

'Has she?' I glanced at her in the driving mirror. Thank goodness we'd moved on to safer topics. 'And who's Belinda? One of your dolls?'

Nikki's tiny nose wrinkled in disdain. 'No, silly! You know! Belinda is married to Joel. Lucas and Charlotte, and Joel and Belinda.'

'Oh . . . I didn't know Joel was — er — married.' There was absolutely no reason why he shouldn't be, of course. It was just that I suddenly found I didn't want him to be. Which was totally ridiculous — especially under the circumstances. 'And does Belinda live at Hayfields as well?'

'No!' Nikki rocked with laughter as we approached the farm. 'She can't do, can she? She's in prison!'

I parked the Mini jerkily in the yard. The three dogs loped up to us, tails wagging, tongues lolling. There was no other sign of life so I guessed that Amanda and Peter were still asleep.

I unbuckled Nikki from her straps and picked up her bag in a sort of stunned daze. The child obviously watched far too much television, or at least I hoped she did. If all this wasn't a figment of her overactive imagination, then I'd just landed myself a job in a scenario that would be a soap opera writer's dream.

'Come and see my room now,

Stephanie,' Nikki shrilled, pushing the huge dogs away with ease as she galloped towards the back door. 'I've got Sindy's magic castle!'

The next few days were wonderful. Nikki was spirited and headstrong and, as I'd been warned, spoiled rotten. But she was also enchanting, mercurial company, and seeing Hayfields and Morton Hassocks and the Matthews family through her eyes was a revelation.

We took it slowly — well it was new ground for us both — but there seemed to be no early problems. She was confident and bright and inquisitive and fun to be with. She was also wildly indiscreet. I had a feeling that if the rest of the Matthews family realised just how much she took in, they'd be very, very careful about what they discussed in front of Nikki in future.

There had been no more mentions of 'Charlotte and Daddy' or the imprisoned Belinda. Okay, yes, I *was* tempted to ask — I'm only human — but thought better of it.

Amanda, delighted that Nikki and I seemed to have struck up an instant rapport, was out of the house each afternoon and most nights because of the play, Peter worked long into the evening and I usually heard him arrive home not long before Amanda did at night, and Joel's appearances were brief but friendly.

Irritatingly, I found myself looking forward to hearing Joel's voice in the kitchen, or finding his jeep parked in the farmyard. I put it down to loneliness . . . Well, that was my excuse. There was absolutely no way that I wanted to become involved with any man — and certainly not a married one.

Anyway, in between taking long walks around Morton Hassocks with Nikki and the dogs, drives to the beach — wild and windswept on the shortening September days — where I relearned the arts of skipping and football, and innumerable teach-me games deep in the cosiness of Nikki's delicious pink and cream fairytale bedroom, I discovered quite a lot about the Matthews family.

Nikki guilelessly told me that Mummy had had her face stretched and had been in hospital and had come home with black eyes but it had been worth it. And that Daddy dyed the grey bits in his hair. And that Lucas took photos for a living but it was a mug's game and didn't pay enough to keep a roof over their heads and Charlotte wanted more money to spend on fripperies. And that Belinda rang Joel nearly every day. And that Daddy sometimes said it was about time Joel found a place of his own to live.

'Why did you come and live here?' Nikki asked one afternoon as we walked along the beach with the three lurchers. 'Don't you have a house of your own?'

'I do — or at least, I used to . . . ' I stared out at the crashing waves as my curls flew wildly round my face. 'I had a flat which I shared with my best friend.'

Nikki's eyes were wide. 'Oh, Stephanie! Haven't you got a Mummy and Daddy, then? Are you like Heidi? Awfulled?'

'Orphaned!' I smiled down at her wide eyes. 'No, nothing like that. I've got a lovely Mummy and Daddy — just like you have. But when I was teaching, I needed to live closer to my school, so I had to leave home, and Lynne needed someone to share her flat and — '

'Is Lynne your best friend?'

'She was . . . ' I spoke quietly. 'Once upon a time . . . '

'What happened to her? Did she die like that poor girl in Little Women?'

I shook my head. 'No . . . and isn't Little Women a bit old for you? Did Mummy read it you?'

'Nah!' Nikki screwed the heels of her trainers into the damp sand. 'It's not a book, silly! It's a video! So, what happened to Lynne if she didn't die?'

'She got married. And she didn't need me as a best friend any more.'

'Because she'd got her husband to be her friend? What is he called? Is he nice?'

'He's called Richard and I used to think he was nice, yes.'

Nikki stopped making her sand patterns. 'So now Richard is Lynne's best friend? Like Mummy and Daddy. And Luc and Charlotte. And Joel and Belinda. And am I your best friend now?' Nikki slid her small hand into mine. 'Am I, Stephanie?'

I smiled down at her again. 'Yes, poppet, I think you probably are.'

★ ★ ★

The rest of September passed in this delightful way, and by the time October arrived with grey skies and winds that howled across the farmyard and whipped the slate waves into white-frothed towers, I felt as though Morton Hassocks had always been my home.

Dangerous territory for someone in my position, I know, but it was such an enclosed and tiny world after the one I'd left behind. It was far too easy to imagine that I was part of this family and always had been.

'You don't seem to have had much time off,' Joel said one evening after Nikki had gone to bed. 'Didn't Ma arrange anything with you?'

We were in the kitchen. I had been making a cup of coffee, looking forward to curling up on my sofa and losing myself in an old Hitchcock film that I loved, when Joel had appeared from the gap between the two cupboards making me jump.

'Yes, she did, of course. One full day a week off — when Peter would be around or she wouldn't be involved in the play,' I said, pushing the milk back into the fridge. I'd actually found my way round the kitchen remarkably quickly. 'And two evenings, or more if it suited everyone — all pretty flexible. She said if you or Lucas were around and I wanted an extra day off then that could be arranged, too. To be honest, I'm not worried. I'm having fun — it doesn't seem like work.'

'But you haven't been out at all. In

the evening, I mean. It's typical of Ma not to notice — she's pretty selfish. Why don't you come down to the Bat and Broomstick tonight? They're having their usual Thursday night pub quiz — you don't have to join in if you don't want to, but you really should get out.'

'What about Nikki?'

'Peter's here, I heard him come in about half an hour ago. He's in the study — pop your head round the door and tell him you're going into the village. He'll be fine . . . '

He was. He looked up from his computer screen and grinned at me and said he was delighted that I'd settled in so well and that Nikki was better behaved with me than she'd been with anyone. He also agreed that of course it was high time I had a night out and that I was to enjoy myself. He had a huge framed photo of Amanda — looking sensational in a bikini — on his desk. I closed the door behind me, convinced that he loved his wife, adored his daughter — and wouldn't risk losing either by playing fast and loose with his step-daughter-in-law.

Joel drove me to the Bat and Broomstick. I hadn't been expecting that to be part of the going-out, to be honest. I'd assumed that he'd be working and that he'd meant for me to drive myself in the battered green Mini.

'One of my nights off,' he yelled across at me as we screamed through the freezing darkness. 'A bit of a busman's holiday, I know — but I love the pub and the village — no point in going further afield.'

I gritted my teeth in a sort of a smile of agreement. The wind velocity made anything else impossible. And I knew, just knew, that by the time we reached the pub I'd have runny eyes and runny nose and hair like Ken Dodd.

As soon as we'd screeched to a halt in the shingle car park, I asked Joel to point me in the direction of the loo, and dashed off to repair the damage. There wasn't a lot I could do, but at least I emerged feeling that I looked a little less like the Mad Woman of Morton Hassocks.

Joel was at the bar chatting to a very pretty barmaid. I wondered fleetingly if I should try to manoeuvre the conversation around to Belinda, but quickly decided against it. Instead I just looked at him — a soft black leather jacket over the rugby shirt tonight, along with the jeans and trainers — and knew that the attraction was now running at danger-level. I gave a little groan of fury. Me, who had sworn to never, ever, ever become attracted to any man again as long as I lived, was now rapidly falling for my employer's married son! Ten out of ten for complete idiocy, I thought.

We got drinks — Joel paid, but only after I'd argued then agreed to get the next round — and found a corner seat by the log fire. The Bat and Broomstick was very olde worlde in a proper village pub sort of way, and everyone seemed to know everyone else. Through a beamed archway I could see a completely full dining area, all dark wood and white candles and silver cutlery, and idly picked up a menu.

'Are you hungry?' Joel asked.

I shook my head. 'No, I had supper with Nikki — I was just interested to see what you cooked — oh, wow!'

The menu was divided up into bar snacks and dining room meals: they were all inventive, unusual and utterly mouth-watering.

'I've been adding different things to the menu for ages,' Joel said. 'Things that Dad taught me to cook when I was a kid, old village recipes, stuff like that. We've got quite a reputation. People come from all over . . . '

I could see that. Nowhere at home would have a pub full of eaters on a Thursday night. 'You must be very proud of all this.'

'It's okay.' He stared down at the table. 'It's what I do — what Dad did before me. I enjoy it.'

'And is your Dad still around?'

'Lives on the Isle of Wight with the woman he left Ma for, running a restaurant. I still see him — Lucas doesn't. The fact that he found more happiness with Bess than with Ma was just one of those things. I really hated him at the time, but understand more as I've got older. When you're a kid you want everything to stay the same for ever — when you grow up you know that it can't.'

'And Amanda — um — your mother — seems happy enough now, with Peter and Nikki . . . '

Joel shrugged. 'I hope so. Luc and I weren't sure about Peter at first — you know, he seemed a real smoothie, a real charmer round women, and Ma's so gullible. Apart from that, as I said, she owns Hayfields — so we thought Peter might be a gold-digger.'

'And now you know that he isn't?'

'Pretty sure he isn't, to be honest. His business is healthy and he contributes plenty of money towards the upkeep of Hayfields. Despite being a bit of a flirt, he doesn't seem to have eyes for anyone but Ma, and she's happy, so that's all that matters. That's how Luc and Charlotte got together, you know, through Peter.'

'Really?' I clamped my teeth on the rim of my glass. I wasn't going to say anything about Nikki's 'Charlotte and Daddy' revelations.

'Charlotte is Peter's secretary. She came up to the farm one day when Peter was working from home and she and Lucas hit it off straight away.'

I beamed. I wanted to punch the air. It was all right. That's why Nikki put 'Charlotte and Daddy' together in the same sentence. That's why she'd seen them together. That's why Charlotte wore her hair down when she was with Peter. At work. It all made perfect sense. No doubt Nikki's Belinda story had an equally plausible explanation.

I reined in the beam, realising that it must look a bit over the top. 'How romantic . . . and how long have they been married?'

'About eighteen months. It's a bit fiery. Luc's a dreamer like Ma and

Charlotte's practical. He irritates her sometimes, I think. Still, I'm the last person to comment on the holy estate of matrimony after all.'

I swear my heart stopped beating. I was holding my breath. This was it! Revelation time. I was going to hear the truth about Belinda and the prison sentence — I just knew it.

# Part Three

'Joel! Just the bloke!' A portly man with a receding hairline towered over our table. 'We're two short on our team for the quiz. You and the young lady have just been voted the couple most likely to help us win.'

Joel grinned. 'You could just be right, Alf. Stephanie is a schoolteacher.'

'Really? Brains *and* beauty — there's a rare treat!' Alf pumped my hand up and down with delight. 'Wonderful — we'll wipe the floor with the opposition. Welcome to the team, Stephanie — you must become a permanent fixture. Come along then, hurry up — we're just going to start.'

I pumped his hand back, and smiled, and muttered that I hoped I wouldn't let them down, but as we grabbed our drinks and coats and I followed Joel across the bar, I knew I might just be embarking on a very dangerous game indeed.

The Bat and Broomstick's pub quiz was great fun. It stretched my brain a good deal and Joel and I laughed and bickered childishly about the answers. We seemed to automatically fill in the gaps in each other's knowledge: I was better on the arts, he knew more about science; I could answer the history questions, he knew all the geography answers. And so on. And the more he teased or complimented me, the more I could feel my defences dropping away.

It had been so long since the days when Richard and I had had this happy bantering camaraderie . . . if we ever had. Somehow, I could only remember the end of the relationship. Those awful days when for some inexplicable reason everything I did was wrong in Richard's eyes, and we argued all the time. Of course, I learned later, that it was his guilt that made him so bad-tempered — but at the time, I'd seriously wondered if I was going mad.

And I'd confided all this to Lynne! Oh, the shame of it now. Those nights in our flat, sharing a bottle of wine, when I'd poured out my heart to her — telling her that I was sure Richard was seeing someone else — never once guessing who the someone else was!

And she'd kept up her deception so well, too. Assuring me that Richard loved me and would never look at another woman. Listening to my tearful ramblings, holding my hand and telling me everything would be all right . . .

Small wonder then, that I'd vowed never to trust anyone ever again.

As I'd almost forgotten how it felt to be at ease in a man's company, Joel's joking friendliness was like a warm blanket on an icy night. Comforting, reassuring, nostalgically familiar. And each time Joel hugged me when we got an answer right it became a little more difficult to remind myself that he was supposed to be strictly off-limits.

By the end of the evening we had come top of the six teams by one point.

Alf was ecstatic and made me promise I'd be there the following Thursday. I said it would depend on my Nannying duties. Joel said he'd see to it, and shrugging into our coats, we headed for the door.

'Damn!' Joel looked at me. 'It's chucking it down. You'll get soaked to the skin in the jeep — do you want to wait here while I drive home and come back with the Mini?'

'No, of course not. It's only a bit of rain.'

We raced for the jeep, heads down against the lashing torrent. The wind had got up too, and was soughing through the bare branches above our heads, and in the distance, the sea was angrily crashing on to the shoreline. I leapt into the jeep, pulling my collar up as far as it would go.

'Hang on, then,' Joel shouted. 'I'll try and get us home as quickly as possible.'

If I'd thought the previous jeep-trips had been hair-rasing, this one was positively white-knuckle. With the blast of the wind and rain punching against us, the forward thrust of the jeep made it seem as though we were driving into a brick wall of sound and motion. Tearing through the darkness, with the rain streaming down my face and the wind making my curls stand on end, and with the added bonus of being thrown against Joel at every corner, I felt young and alive and wanted to laugh out loud.

We reached Hayfields far too soon.

'Look at you!' Joel spluttered with laughter. 'Drowned rat of the year!'

'You don't look any better,' I retorted, grinning at him and trying to unplaster my hair from my face.

I knew my mascara would have run, and my curls would be little corkscrews, but somehow it didn't matter. For the first time in months I felt truly happy. Standing there in the darkness while the violent and freezing storm crashed round us, I realised that the knot of sadness had at last disappeared from beneath my ribs.

We splashed through the porch and dumped our jackets and shoes amongst the paraphernalia of living which had accumulated there. Joel threw open the kitchen door, ushering me inside, scattering raindrops all over the dogs. 'I'll get the kettle on while you dry off. I think this calls for coffee with more than a dash of rum — oh, and Stephanie . . . '

I was heading through the wonderful warmth of the kitchen towards the hall, en route to my room to grab a towel. 'Yes?'

'You don't have to drip right through the house — this is quicker.' And he disappeared into the corner between the cupboards.

It was all very Lion, Witch and Wardrobe, but intrigued, I followed him.

'Oh!'

The gap between the cupboards led to a thickly panelled door, which in turn opened on to a short flight of whitewashed steps which then led up again the other side to another door.

'This was originally the entrance to the farmhouse cellars,' Joel said, unlocking the door. 'You can still get down there through that little door to the right, see? And this,' he pushed the door open, 'was the original Hayfields conservatory.'

I stepped into a fully self-contained split level apartment. There was a huge bed with books and magazines strewn across it and all the latest television and audio equipment beside it. Vast wing chairs, a sofa with deep cushions, and an Indian coffee table were arranged on the upper level, and the whole was encased with ceiling to floor windows. Voile drapes offered privacy, and multicoloured glass beaded curtains reflected rainbow lights as Joel switched on various lamps.

'Kitchen this way — bathroom through there — ' he pointed away from the bedroom area. 'All mod cons. You get dried and I'll make coffee in here shall I?'

I plunged into a bathroom — all black and white and sumptuous — delighted to have discovered Joel's between-the-cupboards secret, but devastated to realise that this was no bachelor apartment.

The bed was double, the furnishings had a feminine touch, and there were bottles and bottles of expensive toiletries in the bathroom . . . Belinda, it seemed, was set to return.

By the time I'd wiped away the mascara dribbles and patted my hair into some semblance of order, Joel had made coffee and was sprawled in one of the wing chairs.

'My turn to get dried. Your coffee's there on the table — biscuits are in the tin — and the rum's in the coffee.'

'Thanks — this place is wonderful.'

'I like it.' He paused in the bathroom doorway. 'It suits me. Luc and I shared it when we were kids — we were the envy of all our friends. Won't be a minute — put some music on, or the telly — just make yourself at home'

Dangerous, dangerous offer, I thought,

picking up my coffee mug and wandering across the beech wood floorboards to mooch through Joel's music selection and his bookcases. I always think you can tell so much about someone by their taste in books and music. Both were pretty eclectic: some stuff I liked myself, some classics, some I'd never heard of.

Just as I was about to treat myself to the Moody Blues Greatest Hits, the phone rang.

'Stephanie! Answer it would you, please?' Joel's voice echoed from the bathroom. 'Otherwise it'll transfer to the main house number and wake Nikki up. Tell who ever it is that I won't be long. It's probably just Luc or someone from the pub.'

I lifted the phone. 'Hello . . . '

'Hi, Amanda . . . ' the female voice was smiling. 'Sorry if this has clicked through to your phone. Is he in?'

'Er . . . Joel, do you mean?'

'Who else? Are you okay? You sound different . . . '

'Oh, I'm fine . . . um — he's just coming . . . who shall I say is calling??'

'Amanda! You'd better be joking! Don't you dare tell me he has a harem of women ringing him at this time of night and break my lonely heart! How's the play going?'

'Oh, er . . . great . . . ' I was withering inside. 'I'll just go and get him for you, shall I?'

I dropped the phone on to the coffee table. I knew who it was. Her voice was warm and friendly and filled with longing. As my only knowledge of prison phone calls was from television dramas, I could visualise her standing there in grey and barren surroundings, in a line of tough-looking women all clutching their allotted phone cards for that vital five minutes of talking to the outside world. Who was I to deny her that luxury?

Joel appeared from the bathroom, still rubbing his hair, and raised his eyebrows. 'Who is it?'

'She didn't say . . . and — um — I

think I'd better go now. Thanks for the coffee..'

'But you haven't touched it — ' Joel looked puzzled as he picked up the phone. 'Hi . . . '

Before he spoke I was opening the door. As I closed it behind me I heard him say, 'Belinda — hello, love. No, it's not too late — I didn't think you'd ring tonight . . . '

I clattered up and down the little steps and emerged into the kitchen. From their beds beside the range, the dogs looked up at me with sorrowful eyes and thumped their tails in sympathy, and as I ran upstairs, the rain lashed ceaselessly against the widows like silent tears.

★   ★   ★

I spent the next few days studiously avoiding Joel. There was absolutely no point in reopening wounds that had just started to heal — or even worse, inflicting new ones. Joel was married, he and Belinda had a lovely home here where I worked, he was my employer's son and had been nice to me out of a sense of duty. That was it. That was all. That was all there would ever be. And after Christmas, when Amanda had finished the play and Nikki started school, I'd go home and begin my life again.

Well, no, I probably wouldn't go home just yet . . . That part of my life was over, too. I'd — oh, I'd take a job on a cruise ship, or become a travel rep or well . . . anything that would take me as far away from memories and Morton Hassocks as possible.

My parents, in our weekly phone calls, had been delighted that I was so happy. I couldn't go home yet and shatter all their illusions, could I?

Nikki, sensing my sadness, had become irritable and awkward. Don't, shan't and won't became her favourite words. The weather had turned perpetually cold and grey, wet and windy, and even the dogs were restless.

Our daily routine of breakfast, television for Nikki while I showered and dressed, then out for the day if the weather was good enough — or if not, my own pet project of restoring the messy living room to pristine glory — suddenly seemed to pall.

'Why don't you take Nikki down to Luc and Charlotte's?' Amanda said one morning. She was flitting around the kitchen, her script in her hands, trying different infections on the same line. It was driving me mad. 'Peter's away at a conference in London today and Charlotte is working from home. Apparently Lucas is taking dreary sepia bad weather shots on the coast for an art magazine, so she'd probably be glad of the company.'

'Yes, okay, it sounds like a good idea.'

'Charlotte might even like a trip into Bournemouth for a bit of retail therapy. God knows, it'd do her good to splash out on something frivolous.'

Probably not if she and Lucas are short of money and she's supposed to be working, I thought, but I didn't say anything. To be honest, a little chat with Charlotte may not be a bad thing.

I'd seen her a lot in company and a few times alone, since joining the Morton Hassocks entourage, and had nearly, each time, plucked up the courage to ask about Joel's marriage to Belinda. Today, I might just mention the late-night phone call and see what happened . . .

No, damn it. I was going to go for the jugular. I took a deep breath. 'Amanda — Belinda rang the other night — I answered the phone. She thought I was you . . .'

Amanda flapped her script. 'I know. Joel told me — quite amusing, actually.'

Amusing? Was the woman mad? I couldn't ask how long they'd been married. I simply couldn't. 'Er — have they known each other for a long time?'

'Oh, yes, for ever.' Amanda stopped pacing and flicked at some crumbs on the bread board. They fell to the floor and she ignored them. 'They went to school together.'

Childhood sweethearts! Oh dear, oh dear . . .

'Have you seen a photo? She's a lovely girl.'

I didn't want to see a photograph. I truly didn't. I wanted Belinda to stay dark and shadowy and hideously ugly in the recesses of my imagination. However, Amanda was scrabbling through a pile of accumulated junk on top of one of the cupboards.

'Joel's got dozens in the flat, of course, but I know there's a lovely one here that Lucas took — ah!'

Apart from closing my eyes, or dashing the photo to the floor, I had no option but to look.

At least it wasn't a wedding shot — but Belinda was still every woman's worst nightmare. A waterfall of silver blonde hair, big blue eyes, a sweet face, full lips, and a huge happy smile. I hated her on sight.

'Very nice — ' I shoved the photo back as though it had scalded me. 'Joel must miss her very much.'

'Oh, yes. It's such a shame that she's away for so long.'

'Away' I thought: so that was the euphemism the Matthews family used. Nikki was chasing her cornflakes round her bowl at the end of the kitchen table so I gathered the shorthand was for her benefit.

'Has she been — er — away — for ages, then?'

'From Morton Hassocks? Oh, about three years this time — .'

*Three years? This time?* You only got about five minutes for armed robbery these days! Belinda must be a serial offender and Lucretia Borgia at least!

Sadly, Nikki chose that moment to declare her breakfast was over and that she'd really like to go and see Charlotte and the cats, so I had no option, as the hired-help, but to comply.

Muffled up in coats, scarves, boots and gloves, Nikki and I trudged across the squelchy farm yard and clambered into the Mini. The trees had been stripped bare by the wind, and their glorious autumn leaves lay in glistening soggy piles along the road. The sky was grey and so was the sea. It suited my introspective mood.

Nikki looked at me petulantly through the mirror. 'Stephanie — I want Mummy to finish doing the play.'

'Do you? Why?'

'So she'll care about me again.'

'Oh, sweetheart — of course she cares about you — she cares about you more than anything else in the world!'

'No she doesn't! Daddy was shouting at her again last night — he said he couldn't find anything! And he said she only cared about her damn play!'

I tried not to smile. 'Nikki, that's the sort of thing grown-ups always say to each other when they're feeling tired and cross. He probably meant he couldn't find any matching socks or something like that, and that your Mummy cared more about the play than sorting his clothes out — which he could do himself, after all . . . It

83

certainly didn't mean that she didn't care about you.'

She surveyed me in the mirror. 'Didn't it? Really, truly?'

'Really, truly,' I answered, glancing at her confused face. 'Your Mummy and Daddy both love you very much indeed. Now, see if you can count to fifty without forgetting thirty seven this time . . . '

Nikki giggled — thirty seven was a bit of an ongoing problem — and started reciting in a monotone. 'One and two and — '

I changed gear as we neared Morton Hassocks' two-pump garage and the lean-to, and decided that perhaps I'd have a word with Amanda about trying not to let Nikki overhear rows in future. After all, she'd been the centre of Amanda's attention all her life, her world had been disrupted enough by my arrival, she certainly didn't need further insecurities.

Lucas and Charlotte's shed looked even less prepossessing than ever on this miserable day. I parked the Mini outside and went through the rigmarole of unfastening Nikki from her straps. Mind you, if Charlotte was up to her eyes in work we'd just have to have a quick cup of coffee and find something else to do. Maybe I could take Nikki into Bournemouth to the cinema. There was probably something she could watch that didn't involve murder and mayhem . . .

All these thoughts were floating through my mind as we slithered up the wet path. All sorts of trivia filled my head these days. Anything that would keep Joel and Belinda out . . .

I rapped smartly on the door.

Eventually it was pulled open a crack, and Charlotte, wrapped in a pale blue dressing gown and with her dark hair tumbling round her shoulders, peered out.

'Hi,' I said cheerfully. 'Sorry to arrive unannounced — but madam here thought it was a good time for a visit and — '

'It's not really convenient . . . '
Charlotte muttered. 'I'm working from
home today and haven't got dressed yet
and the place is a tip and — '

'Daddeeee!!!' Nikki shrieked, pushing
past me and Charlotte, and thundering
into the lean-to.

Charlotte squeaked as the door flew
open, and so did I as I got a ringside
view of Peter standing in the kitchen,
wearing only his boxer shorts.

'Nikki!' I roared, all the years of
teacher training returning instinctively.
'Nikki! Come here! Now!'

Nikki skidded to a halt and stared at
me. Charlotte and Peter both gawped at
me in frozen amazement.

'Nikki,' I dropped my tone to calm
and considerate, although I was shaking
from head to toe with pure anger.
'Come along. We'll come back and see
Charlotte later.'

'But Daddy . . . ?'

'Is busy.' I fixed Peter with a glare,
praying he'd stay silent. 'So is Charlotte.
Come along. Say goodbye . . . '

She wavered for a moment, then beaming happily at Peter, skipped back towards me. 'Are we going to see a film, now?'

I nodded.

'Why did you shout?'

'I'm sorry. I didn't mean to. Say goodbye.'

She did, and Charlotte and Peter, to their credit, managed their answering goodbyes in normal cheery voices. I turned my back on them and made, what I hoped, was a haughty exit.

Then running down the path, almost lifting the rather startled Nikki from the ground in my haste, I then snatched the car door open and thrust her inside. With fumbling fingers, I fastened Nikki into the rear seat of the Mini. 'Hang on a minute, darling. I've just remembered something . . .'

I belted back up to the lean-to and shoved the door open. Charlotte was nowhere to be seen and Peter was standing in the middle of the living room, still in his boxers and holding his suit jacket in one hand and his trousers in the other.

'Stephanie — it isn't how it looks . . . '

'I'm pleased to hear it because it looks as bad as it gets to me. All I wanted to say is that I'll say nothing to Amanda. That's your job — not mine. And I'll try to keep Nikki from mentioning it, too. And I'm not doing this for your sake — only for Amanda's. Amanda doesn't deserve to be hurt, she's been dumped before, she probably wouldn't cope with it a second time. And believe me, I know how that feels — you . . . you cheating, two-timing pig!'

# Part Four

In Bournemouth, Nikki and I went window shopping, followed by lunch in a fish and chip cafe overlooking the brooding slate sea. Then we sat through the Jungle Book twice, and by the end of the afternoon I'd calmed down enough to face the return to Hayfields. If we timed it right, then Amanda would have already left for the theatre and Peter, if he'd come home, would be either ensconced in the study or the living room and I wouldn't have to face him.

Of course, Nikki had wanted to chat about Daddy and Charlotte, so we did in a light-hearted way, and I'd made Nikki promise not to mention it to Joel or Amanda or Lucas.

'Why not?'

'Because it's a secret.'

'*Our* secret?' Her eyes had been like

saucers. 'Just us?'

'Just us,' I'd improvised wildly. 'Like at Christmas when you have to keep the presents a secret . . . '

'Are Charlotte and Daddy getting presents for Mummy and Joel and Lucas, then?'

'Something like that. And we don't want to spoil the surprise, do we?'

She'd shaken her head solemnly. 'It's important having a secret just between us, isn't it?'

'Very important,' I'd said vehemently. 'Very important indeed.'

We hurried back through the late-afternoon gloom towards the car park. My head was in complete turmoil. Charlotte and Peter! Oh — it didn't bear thinking about! And it had brought back all sorts of hideous memories . . .

It had been a similar autumn day — all lowering sky and leaves rustling bleakly in the gutters — when I'd discovered the truth about Richard and Lynne. That was why, I think, that my

temper had flared so uncharacteristi-
cally when I'd yelled at Peter. It had
been Richard and Lynne all over again.

That awful time — more than a year
ago now — was as vivid as if it had
been yesterday,

I'd finished school early one day
— there had been a flu epidemic which
had swept through the pupils, and had
now started to affect the staff. By lunch
time I'd had a raging temperature, hot
and cold shivers, and every bone in my
body ached. All I'd wanted to do was
get home, make a hot drink, and sink
into bed.

Shakily, I'd fumbled with my key in
the lock. The flat was silent. Empty.
With my head thumping, I'd stumbled
through to the kitchen and switched on
the kettle. Lynne wouldn't be home
until six at least, and I knew Richard
was away at a business meeting all day
so wouldn't be calling round. I'd have
the flat to myself, be able to curl up in
bed and wallow in blissful silence.

It was while I was rummaging in the

cupboard for the flu remedy sachets, that I noticed the briefcase propped against the kitchen table. I frowned at it. It looked like Richard's briefcase — but of course it couldn't be. My temperature must be making me hallucinate. It must be someone else's . . . Someone that Lynne was seeing . . . She hadn't mentioned a new man in her life recently, but maybe she hadn't wanted to, knowing how upset I was over the problems in my own relationship with Richard. She was such a good friend . . .

I'd sloshed water onto to the pungent powder in my mug, and stirred it. The rattle of the spoon had made my head shriek with pain. I'd sipped gingerly at the scalding liquid, while freezing shudders trembled through my limbs. What I needed was a hot water bottle . . . Oh, bliss! Snuggled up in bed on this cold and windswept afternoon with a hot water bottle!

I'd laughed when Mum had insisted I took one with me to the flat 'just in case'. I'd sworn I'd never need it — but at the moment it seemed like the panacea for all ills. But where had I put it? I'd tried to remember, my brain fogged by the flu. The cupboard in the hall? Maybe . . . No — Lynne and I had cleared that out for a jumble sale not long ago . . . My bedroom? Perhaps . . . Oh, no! I remembered. Lynne had borrowed it some weeks previously when she'd had raging toothache in the night and had had to wait until the next morning for a dental appointment.

It was probably still in her room. Clutching my steaming mug in one hand, and my thumping head in the other, I'd shuffled painfully towards the bedrooms. Now we'd always had a rule about not invading each other's space, and respecting privacy and all that — and normally I wouldn't have dreamed of setting foot in Lynne's room while she was out. But this was a desperate situation . . . I knew she'd understand . . .

I'd been about to push Lynne's

bedroom door open when I'd heard the voices . . . Was I hallucinating again? Why did that sound like Richard's voice? No — of course it couldn't be. Lynne must have left her television on when she'd rushed out to work that morning . . . I'd started to open the door.

'No, I agree — we'll have to tell her soon . . . ' Richard's voice was low. 'It's not fair to any of us to carry on like this.'

'She knows something's going on . . . ' Lynne's voice was even lower. 'Oh, what a mess . . . '

'I never intended this to happen.' Richard sounded as though he was pacing the floor. 'I loved Stephanie . . . really — or at least I thought I did. But nothing like as much as I love you, Lynne, darling . . . '

Frozen with shock, my teeth gritted together, dry-eyed, I'd shoved open the door.

Lynne was sitting hunched on the bed looking starry-eyed and moon-struck.

Richard, as I'd thought, was standing by the window, gazing at her with slavish adoration. They both looked at me in open-mouthed horror. I think they started talking together, I can't really remember. Everything after that was a blur.

I remembered dragging my stuff from the flat and going home to my parents' house in a completely unreal haze of flu and heartbreak. I remembered the tears and the pain and the total disbelief. I remembered the humiliation and the anger and the sense of total loss, and the knowledge that nothing in my life would ever be all right again.

I remembered just how long the healing process had taken. A healing process that still hadn't been quite complete when I arrived at Morton Hassocks, and one that would suffer a severe setback if I allowed my attraction to Joel develop any further.

And I simply couldn't put Amanda though that pain. She'd already suffered it once, probably as badly as I had.

No-one would be able to cope with it twice.

'Stephanie!' Nikki was tugging at my hand. 'You're not listening to me!'

'Oh . . . sorry, sweetheart . . . ' I shook myself mentally 'I was miles away.'

'No you weren't, silly! You were here! Next to me. Anyway, I was saying — shall we get some sweets to take home for Mummy and Daddy and Joel?'

'Um? Oh, yes — whatever you like . . . '

Sensing my distraction, Nikki danced alongside me. 'It'll be another surprise won't it? Like the one that Charlotte and Daddy are having? But not a secret.' She tugged even harder at my hand as we approached the brightly lit sweet shop. 'I'm so happy that you've come to live with us, Stephanie. Everything is really happy now, isn't it?'

I nodded. 'Of course it is, love. And it always will be . . . '

We pushed our way into the shop and

I really hoped that those words would be proved true. Somehow, though, I doubted it.

* ★ *

My plans for returning to Morton Hassocks at the right time to avoid everyone, for once, all went like clockwork. Once back at Hayfields, there was no Amanda, nor any sign of Peter — although there was a light on in the study so I knew he was at home.

Nikki, who wanted to distribute her bags of dolly mixtures immediately, was a bit put-out when I said it would be better not to disturb Daddy at the moment.

'He's bound to be busy. And you'll see him in the morning — he can have his dolly mixtures for breakfast. Now — let's run your bath and make your supper and you can tell me how much you remember about the Jungle Book.'

Nikki looked at me with four-year-old scorn. 'I remember all of it. Every bit. You must be getting old, Stephanie, if you've forgotten it already!'

I poked my tongue out at her, a childish gesture which made her shriek with glee, and raced her up the flights of stairs to the bathroom.

My ploy to keep her away from Peter seemed to work though, as by the time she'd retold me the Jungle Book story — with several embellishments which Walt Disney would have been proud of — Nikki was so full of Mowgli and his friends that she seemed to have forgotten all about our secret, and had her bath without demur, ate her supper, and went to sleep singing.

I had a bath too, but passed on the supper and couldn't quite rouse myself to the singing. I tried to push all thoughts of Charlotte and Peter from my mind. After all, it wasn't any of my business. My stay here was only temporary. Anything I said could only make matters worse. But I liked Amanda. I knew how it felt to be — well — I knew how it felt . . .

And Charlotte must be mad! Who, married to Lucas, would look twice at the man-tanned Peter? It had to be the money, I thought, drying myself and scrambling into my pyjamas. Charlotte and Luc were broke, Peter was wealthy, and Charlotte had been won over by presents of jewellery and designer dresses and champagne. That was it. It must be the money . . . It couldn't be anything else — but oh, dear . . . how many lives would be devastated by the affair? It didn't bear thinking about . . .

Even an evening of television didn't quite manage to banish Charlotte and Peter from my mind. It was like a film running perpetually on a loop — and with no happy ending in sight.

Much later I was still mulling these things over and making an old-maidish cup of hot chocolate in the kitchen in the hope that it'd help me sleep, when the phone rang. I left it for ages, willing Peter to pick it up, but he didn't, and as Joel was working at the Bat and Broomstick, I lifted the receiver.

'Hi . . . ' Belinda's voice smiled down the line. She had the most smiley voice I'd ever heard. 'Who's that?'

I wasn't going to make the same mistake twice. 'Stephanie. Nikki's Nanny.'

'Oh, right. Hello. We spoke before, but I thought you were Amanda — so sorry.'

'That's okay — you weren't to know. Um — Joel isn't in . . . '

'No, I know it's one of his working nights. I've tried his mobile but it's switched off — as always. I wonder if you could give him a message?'

'Yes, yes of course . . . '

'Tell him I'll be home on Friday evening . . . hello? Stephanie? Are you still there? Did you get that?'

'Yes,' I muttered. 'I got it. I'll tell him then . . . '

'Great. Look forward to meeting you — sorry — got to dash. They don't give you very long! 'Bye!'

I stood looking at the silent phone for ages. I presumed she was getting parole or a home visit — I knew enough from films to realise that this happened. But Friday ... ? The day after next ... Having frenziedly stirred my hot chocolate until it was more froth than anything else, I pondered on the possibility of developing a case of beriberi or anything else that would keep me confined to my room on Friday. Anything rather than have to witness the passionate and touching reunion between Joel and blonde, bouncy, beautifully flawed Belinda.

Leaning against the range, allowing the warmth to seep into me, I sighed heavily. The morning's embarrassing business with Peter and Charlotte, having reawakened so many memories from my past, had also achieved something else.

For the first time I'd been able to relive the whole nightmarish Richard and Lynne scenario and hadn't wanted to cry. The wound was still there, but a scab had formed over the pain, and I knew that as long as I didn't probe it too deeply, there was a good chance it would soon be completely healed. And the reason for this miracle cure was Joel.

I groaned aloud, making the dogs lift their heads and look at me with curiosity. If I wasn't careful, the cure was going to be more painful than the illness! How stupid was that?

Wasn't that simply asking for more trouble? More heartbreak? Joel was friendly, flirtatious, gorgeous — and his wife was coming home on Friday!

'Stephanie! Angel! Goodness — what a night!' Amanda suddenly swooshed in through the kitchen door bringing darkness and cold winds and icy rain with her. The dogs all rushed to greet her. 'Oh, hot chocolate! Scrummy! Be an absolute pet and make me one, will you?'

I did so, because I liked Amanda very much, and also because I suddenly wanted to protect her from the pain that was going to come. She'd subsided into a chair beside the range, still in her theatrical make-up, alternately holding her elegant hands out to the warmth and fussing the lurchers.

'Er — good show tonight?' I asked, handing her the frothy chocolate.

'Wonderful, thank you. Almost a full house again. Oh, I do love all these Noel Coward re-jigs! So glam! I'm having such a lovely time, Stephanie — and it's all thanks to you . . . '

'Well — no — I don't think . . . '

'But of course it is! Nikki is so happy and contented since you came here. And you've taught her so many things. It'll be terrible for her when you have to leave.'

Leave . . . My heart sank. I'd always known I'd have to leave, of course. As soon as the play was over and Nikki went to school — but somehow I'd pushed it to the back of my mind. The thought of leaving Hayfields Farm and Morton Hassocks and the family, and yes, all right, Joel — filled me with the deepest gloom.

I put on my happy face, something I'd perfected well over the last twelve months, and shrugged. 'I'm just pleased that you're satisfied with me and that Nikki is enjoying my company and — '

As in all the best Whitehall farces, Peter chose that moment to make his entrance.

We stared at each other for a fleeting second, a million silent radar messages flashing between us. Then Amanda jumped to her feet and hugged him. He hugged her back, meeting my eyes over her blonde head.

Abandoning my own still-undrunk mug of chocolate on the table I smiled broadly and gave a stage yawn which Amanda would have been proud of. 'Oooh! Sorry — I'm so tired — I think I must love you and leave you. Um — goodnight . . . '

'Goodnight, Stephanie,' Amanda cooed, her face buried in Peter's shoulder. 'Sleep well.'

Peter, who probably knew very well that I wouldn't be sleeping at all, said nothing.

Of course I couldn't sleep. Images of

Peter and Charlotte, Richard and Lynne, and Joel and the gorgeous Belinda, crowded in each time I closed my eyes. And there were more basic physical reasons, too. The fish and chip lunch had been hours earlier, and apart from a handful of Nikki's dolly mixtures, I hadn't eaten anything at all since. Even the hot chocolate had been abandoned.

I tossed and turned in my feather bed, listening to the rain pattering on the skylight above my head while my stomach grumbled, and knew that without something to eat I wouldn't sleep all night.

Tiptoeing to the top of the staircase, I listened carefully. There was no light spilling from the kitchen into the hall, and no sound of voices. Amanda and Peter must be in bed. The coast was clear for an impromptu supper-for-one in the kitchen.

I crept downstairs, still feeling guilty about being ravenous at a time of such high emotional crisis, and willed the dogs to be silent as I made another mug of chocolate and reached for the biscuit tin. I resumed my leaning-against-the-boiler stance, listened to the storm buffeting the solid walls of the farmhouse, and enjoyed my illicit midnight feast. At least now, if I couldn't sleep, it wouldn't be because of starvation.

Just as I was shuffling off with my second mug of drinking chocolate, having shared an entire packet of custard creams with the dogs, Joel arrived home from the Bat and Broomstick.

I really would have liked to have dashed for the hall, but he was in the kitchen before I could make my escape. There was no way I wanted to face him — and especially not in my baggy wincyette pyjamas, shiny faced and flat haired from the bath, and fat as a house after the chocolate-and-biscuit raid.

'Stephanie,' he lobbed his car keys on to one of the dressers. 'Hang on a minute. Have I upset you?'

I shook my head. 'No of course not

— what on earth gave you that idea?'

'Because ever since last week's pub quiz I've hardly seen you, let alone spoken to you, and I thought we were getting on okay.'

'We are, were, you know.'

Why on earth couldn't we be having this conversation when I had full make up on and was dressed in something grown-up and my hair was behaving itself?

Joel frowned. 'No, I don't know. Not really . . . Alf asked me if we were still on for tomorrow's quiz. I said I was, but I'd have to check with you.'

I shrugged. 'Oh, probably not. I can't ask Peter to baby-sit on yet another evening . . . '

'Why ever not? Nikki's his daughter! It's not baby-sitting!'

'Don't shout — ' I glared at him. What he failed to understand was that due to the scene I'd witnessed that morning, I couldn't ask Peter anything, ever, period.

'I'm not shouting.'

'You were.' I tried to hide myself in the darkest shadows of the kitchen so that I wouldn't look quite so hideous. 'And Amanda and Peter have only just gone to bed — and I don't want them to hear . . . '

'Why not?' Joel picked up the discarded hot chocolate mugs from the table. 'Anyway, they won't. The walls are three feet thick. Have you been having a hot chocolate marathon?'

I stared guiltily at the mugs. The custard creams felt like a lead weight in my stomach. He must think me a real glutton. 'They're not all mine. One of them belongs to your mother.'

He laughed. 'It wasn't an accusation. And at least you're speaking to me now.'

'No I'm not.'

'Now you sound like Nikki!'

'Thanks. Infantile, do you mean?'

'No, just funny . . . ' The dogs had hauled themselves sleepily from their baskets and were writhing round Joel's legs, obviously waiting for yet another biscuit tin sortie. 'So what have I done wrong?'

'Nothing . . . nothing at all. It's just — well . . . ' I stopped and shrugged helplessly.

How could I tell him that I thought he was the most beautiful man I'd ever seen — and even more than that, that he was friendly and funny and nice and that he — against all the odds — had cured the pain of Richard's perfidy?

How could I tell him all that when, nice man or not, he may well laugh in my face? How could I talk about love — when his stepfather and his sister-in-law were having an affair — and his mother's and brother's lives were about to be torn apart? How could I tell him any of it? What was the point of anyone ever loving anyone else? It only ever ended in heartbreak.

Joel stared at me, then shook his head. 'Women! I'll never understand women!'

'Fine, then I'll just leave you to ponder on it, shall I? Oh, and — ' Just as I turned to scuttle out of the kitchen I remembered the Number One reason why falling in love with Joel was the worst thing I could ever do. 'Belinda rang earlier. She's coming home on Friday. Good night.'

# Part Five

Part Five

Predictably, on Thursday Hayfields broke out in a fever of excitement over the imminent return of Belinda. To be honest, I felt as though I was starring in a Whitehall farce. There were things I couldn't say to Amanda, or to Joel; I didn't want to see Peter or Charlotte or Lucas; and I lived in perpetual fear that Nikki was going to have one of her indiscreet moments and blurt out everything to everybody. But more than anything at all, I simply did not want to come face to face with Belinda.

Talk about the return of the prodigal. Amanda immediately telephoned the theatre and after much sweet-talking of director and producer, arranged for her understudy to take over for Friday evening's performance.

'We'll have a proper family supper party,' she trilled. 'In the dining room

— which is at least tidy as we so rarely use it. I'll ask Joel to cook all Belinda's favourites, and we'll get Charlotte and Lucas to stay overnight so that we can all have a drink — oh, and I must make sure Peter hasn't got anything pressing on for tomorrow evening and — '

I listened to all this with mounting horror. All those people — all those secrets — all those damn undercurrents — all in the same place at the same time!

Naturally, I didn't go to the pub quiz, which was a shame as I'd thoroughly enjoyed it, and Joel went alone and came back early and slammed into his space between the kitchen cupboards, so I gathered they'd lost. Charlotte had phoned during the evening — I'd had to answer the phone again — just to say she and Lucas would be there on Friday for the welcome home party.

'Oh, and Stephanie . . . '

'Yes?'

'About the other day . . . it wasn't at all how it looked, but I'd still rather that

Lucas and Amanda didn't know any-thing — '

I bet you would, I thought. I sighed. 'You can rely on me to keep quiet. I've already told Peter it's none of my business.'

'Thanks — look, one day I'll explain it all — '

'I'd rather you didn't,' I said frostily and with a lot of self-control if you want to know — because obviously I was dying to hear all about it. 'It has nothing to do with me at all.'

And then it was Friday.

Belinda was arriving at Hayfields at about seven o'clock. Dinner was going to be at eight. Amanda spent all day polishing things that hadn't seen a hint of a duster for years, Joel was cooking up a storm in the kitchen, and Peter was — as ever, even on his day off — locked in his study. Nikki and I, feeling a bit *de trop*, were dispensed to amuse ourselves by 'doing' the dining room.

The dining room was a revelation. As

all the meals I'd eaten at Hayfields had been at the kitchen table or from trays-on-knees in front of the television, it was the first time I'd spent any time in there. The furniture was all 1930s walnut, the curtains were apricot silk, and the rugs were jewel bright and Persian. The dogs, like us, not wanted anywhere else, sniffed everything with interest, and eventually settled down in a huge shaggy heap in front of the cavernous fireplace.

'As it's so cold, we ought to ask Mummy if we could have a proper fire in here tonight,' I said to Nikki who was counting out cutlery on the floor. She still skipped thirty seven. Still, who needed thirty seven knives and forks anyway, I thought.

'We have one in here at Christmas,' she looked up at me, the tip of her tongue protruding between her teeth from the effort of the counting. 'After Father Christmas has come down the chimney. Stephanie?'

'Yes?'

'We've still got our secret, haven't we?'

'We have,' I nodded, groaning inside. I'd hoped she'd forgotten all about it.

'Will Daddy and Charlotte give everyone their surprises tonight?'

Oh, very probably I thought. I rattled around with a clutch of tarnished napkin rings and the silver polish. 'I shouldn't think so, love. Tonight is for Belinda — and Joel . . . We'll have to keep our secret for a bit longer.'

'And will Daddy and Charlotte have to keep theirs, too?'

'Definitely Daddy and Charlotte will have to keep theirs, yes. Now, where does your Mummy keep the candles?'

⋆  ⋆  ⋆

I deliberately headed upstairs for Nikki's room at about three-thirty. Lucas and Charlotte were arriving around five, and I didn't want to see them either. It was also pretty depressing to discover that as it was such a special occasion, Nikki was being allowed to stay up and eat with the grown-ups. I just hoped she'd manage to stay silent.

While she chose which particular princessy party dress she was going to wear, I tiptoed downstairs again. Deciding that being out of the way for the entire evening would be a great opportunity to catch up on my reading, I wanted to snaffle a couple of good romantic novels that I'd spotted in one of the bookcases.

I was on my hands and knees in the hall, riffling along the spines, when Joel came out of the dining room and nearly fell over me.

'Oh, just the person I was looking for . . . '

I wished! 'Really? Why?'

He frowned. 'What the hell is wrong with you these days? No — it doesn't matter — look, the dining room . . . '

'Don't you like it? Nikki and I did the best we could — there wasn't much choice in the gardens — soggy chrysan-themums and a bit of evergreen, but I thought — '

He shook his head. 'The flowers look great. The whole room looks amazing. I didn't even know we had candelabra . . . You'd be a wow at the Bat and Broomstick, you've got a real flair — but it's the place settings. You've laid up for seven.'

'Yes, I know. Amanda said Nikki was having supper with you . . . '

'There should be eight.'

'Should there? Sorry, I must have missed someone. Who else is coming?'

'You are.' He ran his fingers through his short dark hair making it all spiky on top.

I really wanted to shriek with laughter. 'Me? Oh, I don't think so! Why on earth would you want me at a family reunion dinner? Nikki will have Amanda and Peter to keep an eye on her and — '

'But you're part of the family.'

I did laugh then. I'd never heard

anything quite so ridiculous. 'No, I'm not. I'm the paid help. The Nanny.' And very much the odd one out tonight. Having found the books I was searching for, I scrambled to my feet. 'What on earth made you think that I'd been invited?'

'Because I — oh, forget it.'

I watched him crash back into the kitchen and wanted to cry.

★   ★   ★

By six o'clock, Nikki was preening herself in front of the mirror. She'd chosen a dress in silver and gold with matching sandals and was wearing a tiara. A touch over the top for a family dinner, I thought, but as I wanted her to be an angel for the entire evening, I hadn't raised any objections.

'Nikki, are you dressed yet?' Amanda, looking stunning in a long black skirt and a blue cashmere sweater, swept in, 'only Charlotte and Lucas have arrived and Stephanie needs time to get ready.'

For what? Bath and bed? And then to curl up with my books?

'Look, Mummy!' Nikki executed another mannequin twirl in front of the mirror. 'Hasn't Stephanie made me look pretty?'

'She has indeed, darling!' Amanda hugged Nikki then kissed me. 'She looks gorgeous! Thank you — thank you so much for everything you've done.'

Thinking that this sounded a lot like the start of a long goodbye, I pulled a face. 'And I hope I'll carry on doing much the same until the play's finished. I — I love it here.'

'And we love having you. I can't imagine how we managed before you lived here. Now, what are you wearing?'

'Uh?' I blinked. Currently jeans and a baggy jumper, in a moment a bath towel, and after that my ill-famed wincyette pyjamas.

Amanda looked at me as though I

suddenly had trouble understanding basic English. 'For this evening? For supper? What are you wearing? I do so love dressing up, don't you?'

No, I hate it, I thought, and wondered if Amanda had misunderstood the entire situation. 'I — um — didn't think that I'd been invited . . . '

'Of course you haven't been invited. No-one has been invited. It's family only — and you — ' she kissed me again, 'are definitely part of the family. Now, don't worry if you haven't brought anything dressy, come-as-you-are is really the order of the day — it's only me and Nikki who tend to go a little over the top on these occasions.'

I exhaled. As I hadn't declared the symptoms of beriberi anywhere near early enough, and had absolutely no other excuses at all, it honestly looked as though I was just about to spend one of the most nightmarish evenings of my life.

An hour later, dressed in my best baggy black trousers and a white silk shirt — the nearest outfit I had to 'posh' — and with probably far too much eye make up and definitely not enough confidence — I walked slowly down the stairs.

The happy-chattery noise was echoing from the living room. At that moment, I truly wanted to hurtle into the kitchen and hide in the dogs' baskets.

Too late.

'Stephanie! You look gorgeous!' Peter emerged from the living room as I reached the bottom of the stairs. 'Come along in and have a drink. Um — Charlotte and — er Luc are dying to see you again.'

Oh yeah — I bet they are. 'I'm looking forward to seeing them, too.'

'Stephanie — about the other day . . . '

'I have no idea what you're talking about.'

'Thanks . . . '

Our eyes met with mutual understanding.

'I was just going to get some more ice,' Peter glanced at the ice bucket in his hands as though it had just appeared there by magic.

'Let me,' I practically wrestled the ice bucket from his grasp. 'I'm — er — closer to the kitchen than you are.'

He tugged at the bucket for a moment, but it was an unequal struggle. There is no strength like that of a woman who's just spotted a delaying tactic.

Clutching the ice bucket, I clattered into the kitchen. The scents wafting from the cooker made my taste-buds tingle. The dogs, who'd obviously been fed on titbits of would-be dinner party fare by Joel all afternoon, were slumbering in front of the range. I stepped over them and ferreted about in the freezer for the ice.

How long could I reasonably take, here? How long would a normal person take to fill an ice bucket? Five minutes or so, surely? Another five minutes before I walked into the lion's den?

I started chipping away at the long-overdue-for-defrosting-freezer very, very slowly.

'Hey!' Joel's voice made me drop the rescued ice cube trays with a clatter. 'You look great — really lovely. I'm so pleased you changed your mind about eating with us tonight — it wouldn't be the same without you. Oh, sorry — no, let me . . . '

We were both on our knees, scooping up ice cubes.

'Amanda said I should be there,' I muttered, relieved that my curls hid my face. 'She said I was family.'

'You are,' Joel's voice was very close to my ear as we dived for the same recalcitrant ice-cube. 'Or at least . . . '

He kissed me.

I stared at him for one amazing moment, then closed my eyes and kissed him back. As I had handfuls of melted ice, the niceties probably weren't properly observed, but as first kisses went, it was somewhere up there in the stratosphere.

Trembling, I pulled away from him and sat back on my heels. 'Oh, dear . . . '

He smiled. 'Oh dear? *Oh dear?* I must be losing my touch . . . '

I laughed. 'You're not — believe me . . . It's just — '

With perfect timing, as with everything else in my life, the kitchen door flew open and Belinda walked in.

I had a fleeting impression of long blonde hair and long black coat and a huge smile as I scrambled to my feet, tucked the ice bucket beneath my arm like a rugby ball and belted out of the kitchen.

Everyone looked up as I pushed open the living room door. I thought briefly that I must have 'Joel has just seriously kissed me' tattooed across my forehead. However, after the 'hellos' and 'you look lovelies' had been exchanged and Charlotte and I had not made eye contact, it seemed they were far more interested in adding ice to their drinks than questioning the length of time I'd spent in the kitchen.

'Er — Belinda's here.' I muttered to Amanda. 'She's in the kitchen with Joel.'

'Oh, goody. Still, best give them a bit of time together,' Amanda said with uncharacteristic tact. 'They'll probably have a lot of catching up to do.'

Peter was sitting very close to Amanda on the sofa, while Luc and Charlotte were practically sharing an armchair, as Nikki pirouetted prettily between the admiring groups. It all looked as it should be — and I really hoped it would stay that way. Mind you, I was watching the whole scene as though I was in the front stalls at Amanda's play. All I could think of was Joel's lips on mine, and his hands in my hair, and the fact that I was madly, truly, deeply in love with him.

I stared at the carpet and groaned inwardly. Even if the rest of the family were playing fast and loose with their relationships, there was no way on earth that I'd come between Joel and Belinda. I'd have to leave Hayfields . . . Tonight . . . Well, tomorrow at least . . . I couldn't stay here now . . .

'Stephanie!'

'Oh — er — yes?'

I looked up. My gin and tonic was untouched. Lucas was grinning down at me.

'It's time to eat. They've all gone through — you were miles away.'

'Oh, er, yes . . . ' I stood up. 'Sorry . . . '

The dining room looked glorious. The apricot curtains were pulled against the stormy darkness, a huge log fire crackled in the grate and the candle flames danced and flickered.

'You sit here, Stephanie!' Nikki insisted. 'Next to me!'

I sat. Peter and Lucas were at opposite ends of the table, with Amanda and Joel and Belinda on one side, me Nikki and Charlotte on the other. I didn't know where to look.

'Belinda, this is Stephanie, the newest addition to the Matthews madhouse — you've spoken on the phone of course. Stephanie, Belinda has been part of the family for as long as we can remember.'

Belinda grinned and said she'd heard

a lot about me and it was lovely to meet me and that Nikki was lucky to have me looking after her, and I just said hello, and it was nice to meet her, too and how happy I was at Hayfields. Well, apart from asking which prison she was in, or what heinous crime she'd committed, or telling her that I was head-over-heels in love with her husband, there weren't that many topics open to me, were there?

The first course, filo parcels with mushrooms in cream and white wine sauce, was out of this world. I didn't taste a thing. The conversational ball batted back and forth across the table amidst gales of laughter. Joel's hand brushed mine over a joint-reaching for the bread rolls. I snatched mine away. He grinned at me.

Nikki prattled non-stop. So did Belinda. She was funny and witty and friendly. It was wonderfully relaxed, very cosy, very happy — and I wanted to scuttle back to my attic and bolt the door.

Joel and Belinda took the dishes out to the kitchen and said they'd be back in a moment with the main course. I stared at the damask table cloth.

'We saw Daddy without his clothes on in Charlotte's house!' Nikki announced brightly in a conversational lull. 'Didn't we, Stephanie?'

I closed my eyes and prayed for death.

To my amazement both Peter and Charlotte burst out laughing. I opened my eyes. Luc and Amanda didn't seem quite so enthralled.

'Well — not exactly . . . '

On the other side of me, Charlotte sighed. 'I knew she wouldn't keep it a secret!'

'Oh!' Nikki's eyes were huge as she turned and looked at me. 'Oh, Stephanie! It was our secret! Now they won't get their presents!'

'Would someone mind explaining . . . ?' Amanda's voice was icy. 'What on earth does Peter having no clothes on in Charlotte's house have to do with presents?'

'Nothing, really,' I muttered, 'It was just . . . '

Charlotte touched my hand. 'It's okay, Stephanie — I know you've done your best — and I did say that I'd tell you the truth. I had just hoped it wouldn't be yet or quite so public.'

Lucas and Amanda were still completely stony-faced. Peter was smiling.

Charlotte looked at Luc. 'I'm pregnant.'

I spluttered into my Chardonnay. I hadn't even thought about that one!

Amanda was frozen, the only movement being a slight twitch of her lips.

'What? But you can't be — I mean . . . ' Lucas looked as though he was going to burst into tears and laugh at the same time. 'We always said we'd wait and — '

'Accidents happen,' Charlotte smiled gently. 'And I've only just found out — and there were really good reasons why I couldn't tell you and — '

Peter interrupted her. 'The morning of my conference in London, when Charlotte was working from home, I called in to see her to drop off some discs and files, and she'd just done the pregnancy test. She was completely distraught . . . because she thought Lucas wouldn't want the baby . . . '

'Of course I want the baby!' Luc looked as thought the penny had finally dropped. 'I've always wanted children . . . but we always said we can't afford them on my money . . . Oh, Charlotte, darling! This is amazing! The best news in the world!' And he leaned in amongst all the cutlery and kissed her.

'Which is why I've offered Charlotte a partnership in the firm,' Peter said, grinning at them both. 'You will earn good money from your photography, Lucas, one day, but it seemed the best thing to do in the meantime. I know how damn proud you both are about accepting handouts, and Charlotte deserves this promotion on merit.'

'And he came to tell me about it on the very morning that I knew I couldn't take it!' Charlotte broke in, her arms still round Luc's neck. 'I was just so mixed up and unhappy. And Peter insisted that I thought about it and said he had to dash because of catching the train to London and then caught a glimpse of himself in the hall mirror . . . '

'I'll admit I've got used to Amanda looking after me.' Peter squeezed his wife's still-rigid hand. 'I never gave a thought as to whether the laundry was up to date . . . And so I was about to go to one of the most important meetings of the year, wearing an unironed shirt and a suit that looked like I'd slept in it . . . '

All the cogs stopped whirring and clicked into place. I nodded. 'So, when Nikki and I arrived — '

'I was in the throes of morning sickness and ironing Peter's shirt and he was sponging the worst of the creases out of his suit.' Charlotte finished. 'And you jumped to the obvious conclusion — and we couldn't tell you the truth — because well, both the promotion and the baby had come at the wrong time and I hadn't told Luc and — '

I beamed happily at them. 'I'm so pleased. Really, and I'm sure things will work out . . . '

'That means I'm going to be a grandmother!' Amanda seemed to suddenly emerge from her shock. 'Oh, my goodness! How amazing! How wonderful — I think . . . '

We all laughed.

She nodded. 'And of course Charlotte can take the promotion and carry on working because Stephanie can stay on here and look after the baby — and we'll pay the Nannying fees as a grandparental contribution!'

They all beamed at this wonderful on-a-plate solution.

'Oh, well . . . I mean . . . ' I muttered, thinking how blissful it would be to stay at Hayfields, and how impossible now. 'It sounds great but . . . '

The door opened and Joel and Belinda arrived with trays of steaming dishes.

'Charlotte's having a baby!' Nikki announced. 'And Stephanie's going to look after it!'

There were a lot more exclamations of joy and much kissing and joking and congratulations. And the party atmosphere carried on throughout the rest of the meal. I couldn't look at Joel. Or Belinda. At least, I thought, chasing a honey-glazed carrot round my plate, I could look at everyone else now. It didn't help much.

By the time the raspberry mousse was merely a memory, and Peter had gone to sort out coffee and brandy, and Lucas and Charlotte were nose-to nose beside the fire, and Amanda had whisked Nikki upstairs to get the cream out of her tiara, I was left at the table with Joel and Belinda.

Other than clearing away the candles, there didn't seem any other option but to stay put. I was delighted by Charlotte's news. And also very, very relieved that all my misconceptions had been just that. And in any other circumstances I'd have been deliriously happy to think that I'd be staying on at Hayfields for at least the next few years

... As it was, the reasons why I couldn't were sitting opposite me.

I sighed. It was time to start acting like a sensible grown-up person and face reality.

I smiled across the table. 'How long have you been married?'

'I'm not — ' Belinda frowned, 'and Joel isn't — well, at least, not as far as I know . . . '

I bit my lip. 'But — I thought — you were . . . oh, so you just live together?'

'Us?' Joel raised his eyebrows, that gorgeous, gorgeous grin spreading across his face. 'Me and Belinda? What on earth gave you that idea?'

'Well . . . no, I know you don't at the moment, because of Belinda being — er — away . . . but when she comes out of prison, then — '

They both shrieked with laughter.

Belinda shook her head. 'You've been listening to Nikki, haven't you?'

'Well, yes . . . ' To be honest, I couldn't see what was so darned funny here. The fact that they weren't married had given me a little glimmer of hope, but only a very little one . . . 'She said —'

'Nikki is the world's best romancer!' Joel was smiling gently. 'I thought you'd have realised that by now.'

'Yes, but — '

Joel's eyes were creased with amusement. 'Nikki has grown up with Charlotte and Luc being together, and because Belinda's parents have emigrated, she lives here when she's in England. I suppose Nikki just throws us into the same bracket. A couple. Together. Heaven forbid! We're far more like brother and sister. We've been best friends since we were kids.'

'Oh, but — in your flat — there's a lot of — um — girlie things . . . and I thought . . . '

Belinda smiled kindly at me. 'Joel lets me have the run of the flat when I stay here. He thinks I need a bit of privacy. He moves out into the spare room. I — um — always leave stuff lying around. My way of saying that I'll be back I suppose. I do get lonely.'

'And she added the cushions and the pictures and things — ' Joel picked up the thread. 'She says I live like a typical bloke. No refinements . . . But where the heck did the prison bit come from?'

'My fault,' Belinda tucked the waterfall hair behind her ears. 'The last time I was home, Nikki asked me why I only stopped work occasionally, and I said because they kept you locked up all the time — like in prison . . . ' She smiled at me again. 'I'm in the army. My postings have been pretty erratic. Despite Mum and Dad not being here, Morton Hassocks is still my home, but Nikki couldn't understand why I didn't come back from work every night like normal people.'

I felt incredibly stupid! I really, really should have realised.

'I'm sorry . . . ' I played with a few grains of spilled salt. 'You must think I'm completely mad.'

140

'I think,' Belinda said, standing up, 'that you and Joel could do with a couple of minutes, pre-coffee, to have a little chat . . . '

She closed the dining room door quietly behind her.

'I'm so sorry. I've made a complete idiot of myself,' I muttered, blushing crimson and scarlet and vermilion. 'I really should have just asked . . . '

Joel had moved round the table and slid into Nikki's chair. He stroked my cheek. 'I do wish you had. We've wasted an awful lot of time . . . '

'But, I didn't think — I mean, couldn't even imagine that you'd — um — like me.'

He grinned. 'I don't like you. I've never liked you. I fell in love with you the minute I saw you. But as I've got such a bad track record with relationships, I didn't want to come on too strong and frighten you away . . . I was engaged some years ago to one of the waitresses at the Bat and Broomstick . . . She dumped me for the sous chef two weeks before the wedding . . . '

'My ex-fiance married my best friend on the day I came here . . . '

We looked at each other. But not for long. The second kiss was just as stratospheric as the first.

'So you'll be staying on at Hayfields, then?' Joel murmured into my curls, his fingers tightly entwined with mine. 'Even after Ma has finished the play? To look after the new arrival?'

'It looks as though that's the plan, yes . . . '

He nodded, his face against mine. 'I just wondered if you'd consider moving?'

'What? But I love Morton Hassocks and Hayfields — and you . . . '

Joel kissed the tip of my nose. 'Thank goodness for that. And actually, I wasn't anticipating you moving very far. Just down about four flights of stairs. From the attic to the conservatory flat . . . '

We do hope that you have enjoyed reading this large print book.

Did you know that all of our titles are available for purchase?

We publish a wide range of high quality large print books including:
**Romances, Mysteries, Classics**
**General Fiction**
**Non Fiction and Westerns**

Special interest titles available in large print are:
**The Little Oxford Dictionary**
**Music Book, Song Book**
**Hymn Book, Service Book**

Also available from us courtesy of Oxford University Press:
**Young Readers' Dictionary**
**(large print edition)**
**Young Readers' Thesaurus**
**(large print edition)**

For further information or a free brochure, please contact us at:
**Ulverscroft Large Print Books Ltd.,**
**The Green, Bradgate Road, Anstey,**
**Leicester, LE7 7FU, England.**
**Tel:** (00 44) **0116 236 4325**
**Fax:** (00 44) **0116 234 0205**

*Other titles in the*
*Linford Romance Library:*

## LOVE'S DAWNING

### Diney Delancey

Rosanne Charlton joins her friend Ruth and family for a holiday in Southern Ireland. Unfortunately, the holiday is marred for her by the arrival of Ruth's brother, Brendan O'Neill, whom Rosanne has always disliked. However, Brendan's presence is not Rosanne's only problem . . . Trouble and danger close round her, like an Irish mist, when she becomes unwittingly involved in mysterious activities in the bay — and finds herself fighting for survival in the dark waters of the Atlantic.

# BETRAYAL OF INNOCENCE

## Valerie Holmes

Annie works hard to keep her father from the poorhouse. However, she is wracked with guilt as she watches her friend, Georgette Davey, being used by Lady Constance. Annie longs to escape her life at the Hall, taking Georgette with her — but how? The arrival of the mysterious doctor, Samuel Speer, adds to her dilemma as Annie's concern for her friend grows. Georgette's innocence has been betrayed, but Annie is unaware of the threat that hangs over her own.

# THE RELUCTANT BRIDE

## Dorothy Purdy

Christine is forced into marriage with Adam Kyle, a wealthy and handsome entrepreneur whom she despises, in order to save her late father's reputation. At first Christine wants nothing to do with him; she tells him she hates everything he stands for. But during their honeymoon in the Friendly Islands her opinion of him changes, and she realises that she has misjudged him. Now she no longer feels embittered, true love blossoms among the sheltering palms.